# Mr. Either/Or

A Novel in Verse

Also by Aaron Poochigian

*The Cosmic Purr* (Able Muse Press, 2012)
*Manhattanite* (Able Muse Press, 2017)

# Mr. Either/Or

A Novel in Verse

Aaron Poochigian

Etruscan Press

Etruscan Press
Wilkes University
84 West South Street
Wilkes-Barre, PA 18766
(570) 408-4546

www.etruscanpress.org

Published 2017 by Etruscan Press
Printed in the United States of America
Cover design by Carey Schwartzburt
Interior design and typesetting by Susan Leonard
The text of this book is set in Arno Pro.

*First Edition*

17 18 19 20 5 4 3 2 1

Library of Congress Cataloguing-in-Publication Data

Names: Poochigian, Aaron, 1973- author.
Title: Mr. Either/Or : a novel in verse / Aaron Poochigian.
Description: First edition. | Wilkes-Barre, PA : Etruscan Press, 2017.
Identifiers: LCCN 2017004994 | ISBN 9780997745528 (softcover)
Classification: LCC PS3616.O625 M7 2017 | DDC 813/.6--dc23
LC record available at https://lccn.loc.gov/2017004994

Please turn to the back of this book for a list of the sustaining funders of Etruscan Press.

This book is printed on recycled, acid-free paper.

For my parents, Don and Toni Poochigian.

I had lived my life one way and could as easily have lived it another. I had done this, not that. I hadn't done one thing, but something else. And so?

Camus, *The Stranger*

# Mr. Either/Or

My special thanks to Bill Schneider and Pamela Turchin.

# Mr. Either/Or

A Novel in Verse

Aaron Poochigian

# Part I: A Cinch

*His Thrice Most Holy Highness Lo-min Wu,*
*Offspring of Heaven, blasphemed when he heard*
*the last gate crashing inward. He was through—*
*poor everywhere were smashing statues of him;*
*soldiers bound by oath to dread and love him*
*cursed his birthday from the burning towers;*
*and now his eunuch court refused to gird*
*its loins for war.*
*Why fight? he thought, why live*
*when all mankind is unappreciative*
*and vulgar? Best to die, but not before*
*he made quite sure the cache of nasty powers*
*he had amassed throughout his thankless reign*
*would not empower some mongrel emperor.*

*So he enchalked a circle on the floor,*
*reached out with words and dragged a ghost, a Gwai,*
*writhing from Hell Nineteen. At his behest*
*the thing sucked evil out of phoenixbane,*
*ox-headed zombies, idols from Cathay,*
*banshee damnations, and The Demon Mare*
*and spat it all inside a carved jade chest*
*known as the Dragon's Claw.*
*The moment after*
*his last man galloped out the gate to bear*
*this plague to safety in the Mongol West,*
*Wu ran a cashmere sash around a rafter,*
*tightened a slip knot, and upset a chair.*
*No one was sad to see him hanging there.*

*Centuries came and went, millennia,*
*but there's no record of the Dragon's Claw*
*until the chronicles of King Wan-Li:*
*the same jade chest displayed at court again*
*as "King Wu's Casket of Catastrophe"—*
*admired, feared, stolen away.*
                              *Since then*
*four hundred modern years have said their say,*
*scholars dismissed its mystic history*
*as folklore, fable, fiction,*
                    *but today . . .*

Washington Square, playground of NYU,
and you are in the grass, your shoes and socks
like sloughed snakeskin around you. Speed-chess players
at concrete tables cuss and slap their clocks
as cops with nothing nine-one-one to do
roust dormant derelicts from greenhouse layers
of coats and trash. Nearby, a Ginkgo tree,
and under it a blonde in horn-rimmed glasses
eating up *The Stranger* by Camus.

You almost feel at home in this milieu;
for five years now you have been skipping classes,
tipping beers and averaging a 'C'
to mask your hazardous identity,
the wicked one, known only to a few
code-numbered codgers in the F.B.I.
Somewhere at Quantico a dossier
redacts your selfless service as a fly
collecting wide-eyed snapshots for Defense,
a freak inferno burning evidence,
a ricin prick, a 'beddy-bye' bouquet,
and all too often the unlucky guy
sent in the long last seconds of suspense
to snip the ticker and defuse a war.

Who knows? Someday it might be nice to play
one person, but for now you live as two:
student and agent, Mr. Either/Or.

Your cell starts bellowing as if on cue,
and the ringtone, the theme to *Peter Gunn*,
can only mean Director "Uh Oh" One,
your handler since you signed for Covert Ops.

"Talk to me, *maestro mio*. What's the word?"

"Tarnation! Kid, this latest caper tops
even that Roswell mess. You ever heard
of Wan-Li?"
        "Nope."
            "The Dragon's Claw?"
                    "Duh . . . no."

A wind-up pause; a cough—here comes the pitch:

"Welp, long about four hundred years ago
Gaspar Van Raadsel, this absurdly rich
nut of a Dutchman, sailed from port Manhattan
(old New Amsterdam) to port Peking.
Then, after swapping cotton socks for satin,
porcelain, oolong tea, that sort of thing,
he paid respects at the Forbidden City,
kowtowed a quick farewell, and shipped at dawn.

The mess he left astern, though, wasn't pretty:
Emperor Wan-li raised a foofaraw
because some hoodoo called the Dragon's Claw,
some nonsense in a carved jade box, had gone
missing. (You'd think the stuff was devil-spawn,
fire and brimstone, lightning, shock and awe,

the way their goddamn Grimoire rambles on.)
Welp, when a culprit never came to light,
the Ming were sure as shit that blatherskite
Gaspar had up and run some Dutchy con,
swiped it from under the Imperial nose
and sailed for Gotham.
                    So the legend goes,
and that was all it was until last night
I get this call—Heinrik Van Raadsel, heir
to old Van Raadsel's fortune, telling me
he's got the damn thing at his pied-à-terre
on Hellgate Hill. Seems Heinie and his noble
forebears never mustered nads enough
to pop the padlock. There's a curse, you see,
squiggles along the lid foreboding global
hell and all if jimmied. One big bluff,
but what's inside? If not the end of days,
some musty bio-weapon?
                  Anyways,
he wants us Feds to take it off his hands.
There have been threatening phone calls, gruff demands
he cough it up and pay some silly fee.
We traced the calls back to a Maoist gang
known as the Righteous Fists of Harmony,
big boys in Chinatown. They make their money
off cocaine and this cathouse called The T'ang . . .
you know it? Yeah, well, don't get any funny
idears.
        Listen: all you gotta do
is march ol' Heinie and the merchandise
downtown to Warehouse Delta. Ninety blocks.

And, kid, do NOT go rooting for the prize
hidden in this particular cereal box—
whatever might be in there ain't for you.

Course, our already strained and fraying ties
to China mean this little interview
ain't never happened. Son, you on your own."

The twang has twangled, so you close the phone.

A gang of grackles chuckles when your boss
texts you the target address: quite a run.
The Free World's grumbling martyr, you uncross
your numbness, brush off grass, and check your gun.

Bare-legged girls are laughing in the sun
as bearded buskers noodle on a nicked-up
cello, bouzouki, and accordion
beneath the arch that Frenchifies the quad.
*Laissez les bons temps* rule. You should have picked up
trombone, you should have mastered being chill.
Too late. You hail a taxi with a nod,
mutter coordinates on Hellgate Hill,
and settle into backseat reveries:
*soft jobs are rare, and this should be a breeze—*
*just ding a doorbell, curtsy, drag and drop.*
*That box . . . that box, though.*
                              As you coast up Third,
Trump Palace pokes its crenellated top
over boutiques and consulates. You've heard
this zone's old money and celebrities—
Madonna, Bono, CEOs of style
in later age. (You don't get up here much.)

The cabbie drops you at a grand old pile
of brass and travertine with ivied eaves.
Rose bushes edge the miniature yard,
and pairs of gimp or headless sphinxes guard
the walkway to the stoop. The door is Dutch,

rough-hewn and bossed, and there's a family crest
above it—Hermes, like, the god of thieves
and Wall Street, holding out a treasure chest.

You pump the buzzer. *Nothing.* Then a blind
bends in a window. Footsteps pad a floor.
The tarnished peephole winks, and half a door
concedes a crack.
                              "Mister Van Raadsel?"
                                                            "Yes?"
"Pleasure to meet you, sir. I've been assigned
to guide your person and a certain box
urgently elsewhere."
                              "Oh, well, yeah, I guess."

A bald and beanbag-bellied codger wearing
a lime kimono and athletic socks
emerges. After several seconds staring
you up and down, he grunts twice, satisfied
your spiel was sterling.
                              Once you squeeze inside,
he only fastens maybe twenty locks
before he turns, begs pardon for the glaring
mess of the place, and leads you to a room
that reeks of Henry Higgins, Sherlock Holmes,
the whole fraternity of bachelorhood.

The furnishings are swimming in a fume
of pipe smoke—sofas, afghans, varnished wood,
forests of it, displaying faded tomes,
chess pieces, ships in bottles, porcelain
two-headed dragons, and a chipped Ming vase.

A bear rug points you to a fireplace
and what must be the master thief himself
posing in oil on the mantel shelf—
Gaspar Van Raadsel, his vermilion grin
like schadenfreude in a black Van Dyke.
Not hard to figure what the jerk was like.

Cracking a wet bar set into the wall,
the heir inquires,
                    "Four Horsemen?"
                                        "Thanks, but no,
not on the job. It's Federal protocol.
Respectfully, we kinda oughta go."

He slams the cupboard shut and snaps, "Alright,"
stomps to a dresser and removes a small
jade chest, a live one, emanating light,
fluorescent light, like an aquarium,
the planet Neptune and a cat's eye all
swirled together. You can feel it hum.

*Whump, there it is, out of the land of fable—*
*the Dragon's Claw, the key to Kingdom Come.*

He sets it gently on a claw-foot table
and hovers, lizard-tinted, in the glow.
A pudgy finger grudges:
                            "See that there?
Those squiggles of calligraphy are *Woe*
*to him who holds me, for beneath my lid*
*dwells desolation.* Quite a little label.
I was a kid when I inherited

this cancer. School was hell enough to bear
and then, *blam*, suicide, my dad was buried,
and his nightmare was mine. I stashed it under
a mound of *Playboys* in the basement closet
and said "hello, monastic life." No wonder,
I mean, you think I could have gotten married
knowing my first-born son would end up cursed
in turn? It's *yours* now. Touch it—that's what does it.
You gotta swear, though, swear to choke back all
desire to crack the lock and peek in or . . . "

Abrupt puffs interrupt him. Windows burst.
Gunfire! Silencers! You hit the floor
on instinct but your host's too slow—a slug
explodes his forehead, brains Rorschach the wall.
Bringing up something like a last guffaw,
he shrugs, then crumples to the bearskin rug
beneath the ruffed and Rembrandt ancestor
who left his family the Dragon's Claw.

*Stay for a stand-off?*
                         Stupid talk.
Dutchie's dead,
                 and duty dictates
you steal his stash.
                     Stuffing your backpack
with contraband that houses
                             horrors, perhaps,
or an antique scam,
                     you scout escape routes.
Hope's out back:
                   where blind bullets
shot up the sunroom,
                      shattered glass doors
frame a plush
                 paradise of produce.

An Olympian lunge,
                     and you land mashing
sweet potatoes.
                 Slats of slanted
latticework lift
                 your velocity over
a ten-foot fence,
                 and trash-bags greet
your lengthwise *splat.*
                   Spoiled seafood
nukes your nostrils,
                 but now's no time
to gag and grimace:

                    gung-ho gunmen
have rushed the alley.
                    Up instantly,
you trust in your All Stars,
                         your track training,
but that weird weight
                    whacking your backside
shrinks your stride
                    and saps stamina.


There's hope, though, *Hoo-ah!*,
                         half a block on:
sun-lit signage
                    for a subway station.
One leap from street level
                         to the lower landing,
and you start stumbling
                    but stay standing.
Parades of posters
                    rush up and push
iPhones, action flicks,
                         online degrees—
*Interminable tunnel!*,
                    and the tough guys hunting you
keep closing.
                    Clips of silenced
potshots purring,
                    pocking concrete
before your feet,
                    you're fucked, man, finished
until a heartening
                    headwind howls in:
by the grace of God,

                    a getaway train.

You hurdle a turnstile,
                    then hide, hunched down,
amid a cluster
                    in the closest car.
*Ding*, then, *dong*,
                    the doors have met,
and rescue is rolling.
                    You rise and smile,
straining to strike
                    stoic straphangers
as, no, not a nut,
                    a normal person.

Focus, freak.
                    Finish the mission.
You lucked out, sure,
                    but this line runs local
the wrong direction
                    and reeks like someone
soiled himself.
                    Screw mass transit.
Once clear of the catacombs,
                    you can catch a cab
down to the Village,
                    dump, daintily,
Armageddon
                    or whatever it is
at Warehouse Delta
                    and unwind somewhere.

Your mind is drifting

                        toward dives and dartboards,
warm waitresses,
                        when *Whoosh!,* an emergency
exit opens.
                Outside air
ruffles coiffures.
                        Fucked-up features
peek in, pug-nosed,
                        pugilistic—
one of the goons,
                        his gun a growth
in pleated pants.
                        Puke must have breached
the next doors down
                        and now is naughtily
crossing cars,
                a crime in this town.


Vlad your Glock
                is getting giddy,
but shots can sheer
                in shaky surroundings,
blast bystanders.
                It's bad news causing
collateral damage.
                Don't yet, dumb-ass;
chill till chance
                chooses a path.

Waiting, you're whistling,
                weighing angles
when a curve kicks
             the car to larboard.
Physics forcing
         freight straight on,
you all sway starboard,
           and the start startles
your instincts to action:

           on the upswing
back to balance,
        you bum-rush Ugly,
check him hard,
        hack his Heckler
across the car.
      *Cough*, though, *gasp*,
he bounces back
        as a black-belt champ
of duck and parry,
         pooh-poohing punches
like last year's fads.
        Feints, footwork,
and your mouth is mashed.
          A meat mustache
sprouts, spreads,
        and the split-lip smacks
of old pennies.

At your eyes' edges
aghast grannies,
                    grinning fiends,
and hipster camera phones
                              clicking close-ups.
Stung by stardom,
                    you sound a wounded
bellow, bear-hug
                    the ballet dancer
against a grab-bar
                    and go gangbusters
kneeing his nuts.
                    Neutered, his resistance
coughs and crumples.
                    Kicks quiet him.


The train slackens,
                    slithers to a station.
Your fans file out.
                    Some few may tell
Metro popo,
                    but most migrate
to the car next door.


                    This kid, though, creeps up—
fifteen, sixteen,
                    his septum sporting
stainless-steel hoops,
                    his hair a hennaed

mess of dreads.

An admirer . . . maybe?

What's he want? Change?

A chance to be champ?

When you bark, "beat it,"

the brat shoots you

a sweet-ass smile

and swipes your backpack.

*Honk, honk*—a hundred twenty-fifth and Lex
(where Central Harlem meets the Barrio),
and you are hungry, cranky, winded, slow,
chasing a little rascal past Tex-Mex
cantinas, soul food joints, and cheap Chinese.

You holler,
　　　　"Kid, I got some money . . . please,"

but, deaf or not, he's dumb to your entreaty.
What can you do? The human jumping jack
surmounting dogs and cabs, all sorts of streety
impediments, you lumber after him
up alleyways into a cul-de-sac
decked out with swing sets and a jungle gym.
Teenagers sporting scarlet tees and black
ball caps are in there practicing graffiti
on garbage cans. They greet their buddy back
with hoots and slaps, then turn and scowl your way.

It's bad, but not that bad. You know this gang.
Crimson and sable means the Broad Day Shooters:
masters of handshakes, architects of slang,
dealers in scrips and nickel bags, freebooters
of bicycles and bongs, which is to say,
a pretty normal horde of adolescents
stuck in the hood with nothing else to do.
Still, even kids can pack a piece or two,
and their demeanor says they find your presence

luscious as dumpster juice. The sitch is such
that you don't want to stir them up too much.

"Nice day out, ain't it?"
                              What would be their king
steps forward, massive in his tasseled leather
vest and vast concatenated bling.
He doesn't want to talk about the weather;
nope, he's fixed on swagger. After winking
back at his boys, he roars:
                              "What *was* you thinking?
Or was you? Fool, you done a wicked dumb thing
playing the pig and snuffing round round here.
You could get beat or stuck or capped or something.
Make like the ghost you are and disappear."

How should you play a teenage gangster's pride?
Dangle a payoff? Scowl and stand your ground?
Whip the indignant Glock out of your drawers
and wave it wildly till you get what's yours?

While you are stuck there struggling to decide,
a rival troop of Boy Scouts scuffs around
the brownstone bend and blocks you from behind:
maroon bandanas flattening the bangs
over their eyebrows, gaudily designed
t-shirts depicting wolves with vampire fangs—
these are Los Lobos Locos, L. L. L.,
least personable of the Latin gangs.

Oh man, these kids are gonna brutalize
the shit out of each other, war like hell
over a playground and its clientele.

You run for cover as, with battle cries
of *suck this, bitches* and *you sons de putas*,
the enemies collide: the so-called Shooters
swinging chains, pry bars, and baseball bats;
the Wacky Wolves all extra-long screwdrivers,
boxcutters, duct-tape shivs, and kitchen knives.
You see forearms at funny angles, tats
bisected, Glasgow smiles, a totaled face.
IVs will soon be nursing the survivors,
and priests insisting boys that lose their lives
fly up and settle in a better place.
(Solace is sweet, but here and now the thought
that someone up there hearts the human race
has never reeked more like a bunch of rot.)

After disco-dancing through a dense
discord of limbs, you apprehend the snot
that robbed you, throw him up against a fence
and grab the backpack.
                                    "Beat it. Go on home."

He beats it, and you bob and weave your way
back through the alley to a parking lot.

Good job, no prob, you have redeemed the day
until, all whining torque and winking chrome,
a dozen motorcycles close around you,
the riders' pistols leveled at your head.
The hunt you shook downtown has up and found you.
How, though? Maoist pricks must have been fed
surveillance footage from the train and street.
Outmanned, outgunned, outspied—there's just one play

to make, and so you make it, bow and lay
the jade-chest-laden backpack at your feet.
When one of them eclipses lines of fire
to come collect the jackpot, that's your cue—
you juke left and recover, shoulder through
astonished goons and duck behind a tire
jutting from a flatbed semi-trailer.

No shouts, no shots. Now that they've won the prize,
the hornets rev and buzz back toward the hive,
and you are left there, stung but still alive,
insisting, no, no, you are not a failure,
you're gonna get the box back, gonna kill those guys.

# Part II: Girls Against Boys

The Met Museum. Panes of glass like ice
preserve a glossy parchment mashed from rice
and, on it, facts a Taoist brotherhood
dignified with calligraphy:

       *. . . the day*
*King Wu the Wicked conjured up the Gwai,*
*he also ordered it to suck the good*
*properties out of prayer-wheels from Tibet,*
*home-scrolls, moonstones, heartsvine, and aloeswood*
*and spit them all inside a statuette*
*shaped like a Phoenix.*
      *So, at Wu's command,*
*a second rider charged out of the stalls*
*and headed westward, clutching contraband.*
*The riot faded, and the road grew dim.*
*At daybreak wilderness surrounded him,*
*li after li of wolves and waterfalls.*
*Soon forest turned to foothills, plum to pine.*
*A pure-white ibex, as if by design,*
*leapt out and led him like a sacred guide*
*to where a monk cried, "Alms!" (This was an omen.)*
*So the enchanted statue found a home in*
*an unimportant little wayside shrine.*

*Snow fell, then blossoms. When the hermit died,*
*a lotus opened at the cistern's edge*
*while gibbons whimpered from the Gingko trees.*

*Clematis wreathed the Phoenix wings, and hoary*
*mugwort sheathed the talons. By degrees,*
*weevils and winds consumed the hermitage.*

This was dismissed as just another story.

You are the man, but not quite *everything*
that happens in this world belongs to you.
Right now, in fact, outside your point of view,
a fussy art historian named Li-ling,
Li-ling Levine, is cussing as she places
corrected copy for a Late T'ang necklace
back in its bracket. (She will axe the reckless
undergrad who classed the piece as 'Ming.')

Monday, the Met Museum's Asian wing,
and she is primping objects in their cases,
eying, aligning, looking deathly lean
beneath a charcoal blouse. Her pencil skirt
back-slitted, liver, and below-the-knee,
her footwear loud of heel and squeaky-clean,
the whole ensemble labors to assert
*I'm young, but you don't want to mess with me.*

Bachelor's from NYU at seventeen,
a Harvard Doctorate by twenty-three,
she rules her galleries with dainty fist.
Precision. Elegance. Yes, her analyst
keeps harping on some nonsense called 'regression
in service of the ego' (that is, 'play'),
but who has time for Scrabble? Her profession
is husband, lover, habit, and obsession,
and there are too few hours in a day.

So she continues poking into nooks
and vitrines, tap-tap-tapping the parquet,
until an odd sight ruffles her routine:

a statuette, a faience Phoenix, looks
impossibly aglow, the ancient clay
lit from within. Why would a figurine
just all at once start acting out this way?

Before she can appraise this strange occurrence,
noise erupts from the adjoining room:
smashed lacquerware, some magnate's gift in shards
dispersing. It will take more than a broom
to clean that mess up, more than art insurance.

Someone deserves the guillotine, but who?
The doors are locked today. No docents, guards,
or bumpkin tourists, so . . . the cleaning crew?
All that she sees are pots, a busty pair
of Bodhisattvas, a terracotta dancer.
*Who's there? Who's there?*
No answer.

More peeved than panicked,

                              she pounds parquet

out of the Arts

                of Ancient China.

Lions lounging

                on low pedestals

flank the foyer

                to the faux Ming Study,

their trance unbroken

                    as she taps between them.

An American Monday

                  mopes inside:

scant sun through the skylight,

                      obscurity merely

graying gloom.

              A goldfish pond

frets beneath

            artificial falls.

Stone-carvings meant

                to spark transcendence

are terrors now,

              grotesque mutations

impaled on bases.

              Bits of a burst

faience Confucius

              further fragment

beneath her heels.

              *Who mishandled him?*

*Who's lurking about?*

                    Legs taut, she listens,
catches under
              the cascade's cackle
males murmuring.
                Mace and Maglite
two floors down
              in a Tory Burch tote,
she's still got guts
               and growls in greeting,
"Come out, cowards."

                A corner duly
shoots forth shadows,
               shapeless at first,
then humanoid
            with heads of hosiery.
Their grabs are gloved,
               the gauze that gags her
spiked with stupor.

               Stubborn streak
tamed for a time,
            a top sinologist
is trucked downtown
             for a dead-end date
with Maoist spies—
            spicy stuff
cooking outside
           your closed consciousness.

You suck, man. Heaven only knows what terror
has fallen to the heirs of Fu Manchu,
because you suck. Yeah, sure those guys were tough,
tech-savvy bastards, total pros, but you
got sloppy and were way off spy enough.
Failure, you failure, you were born in error.

Hold on, though, was your tantrum just a bluff
back when they ruled you'd fail to follow through
in school and life because of ADD?
Hell no. You said, though bored by boring stuff
like poems, algebra, and broccoli,
you lock on objects sexy to pursue,
go superman and shut the static out.
Look sharp, now, killer; prove what you can do.

　　　　* * *


The T'ang sits under a decrepit El.
Its signage, a colossal blinking hand,
telegraphs what the place is all about.
No shame, no subtlety. The boys in blue
probably pop in often and may well
be shielding the supply for their demand.
(How perfect: greased palms, kickbacks, pay for play,
and Wall Street only seven blocks away.)

You step into a sort of waiting room.
Tea lights adrift in glass bowls cast uncertain

shadows on plush, florid divans. The fume
of sandalwood hangs thick, and through the haze
you notice Chairman Mao is standing guard
over an archway with a beaded curtain.

A Chinese girl behind a desk surveys
your t-shirt, jeans, and sneakers, snaps her gum
and scowls. Her sharp voice jars with the décor:

"You come for rub? Is forty, sweet then hard,
or happy touch for hundred money more."

Like usual, your mouth goes off. A phrase
leaps from your lips, and further details come
tumbling after to complete the lie:

"No time for games . . . You know as well as I
the tide has turned. Imperialist collapse
is weeks away. The glorious underclass
will soon rise up, and in a vengeful manner.
We need to rally round the great red banner
of Mao's decrees, start training and amass
our stockpile. Comrade, I have heard, perhaps,
you might supply a weapon for the cause?"

Time dawdles to indulge the awkward pause.
She blows a bubble. More long seconds pass.
Pop, then, and all is changed: she strikes a pose,
wiggles her assets, purrs, "sir, right through here,"
and saunters toward the curtain.
                                        How sincere

is this seduction? Where's she leading you?
Likely a Venus fly-trap, but who knows?
Not every blessing's too good to be true.
Not every femme's fatale, and you might lose
your best shot at the Fists if you refuse.

Onward it is, then. You pursue your guide
under the portrait, through a shower of beads,
into a narrow hallway that recedes,
it seems, forever. Doors on either side
wear numbers, one through God-knows-what, and bare
bulbs hiss and flicker at rosette, prewar
wallpaper. Weren't you here, somewhere, before?
A roach motel? A hostel? A nightmare?
Your hostess's hypnotic saunter only
heightens the sense of existential gloom—
every knob a cop-out, every room
a land where people go to feel unlonely
for half-hour slots.             The Tunnel of Despair
terminates at a suite which, you assume,
is set aside to serve some special use.
She turns a key and parts the doors, revealing
a master bedroom, but without the bed.
There is a kind of dentist's chair instead.
The walls are burgundy, the carpet puce,
and sagging 'funhouse' mirrors on the ceiling
show you yourself at sea in shades of red.

Your escort gathers towels from a rack
and nods to the recliner. You obey.
One crank, and you are laid the whole way back,
eying your puffed reflections, feeling gay.

You try to master your embarrassment
by getting down to business:
                              "Tell me more
about this crew of yours, the Righteous Fists."

No cringe, no gasp. She simply reaches for
a pastel perfume bottle, winks, and mists
the air about you with a frou-frou scent—
lychee, peach blossom, sandalwood and . . . Shit!
your hand, your hand, why can't you wiggle it?
Why are your muscles melting? Why's a bubble
carrying off your thoughts? It's knock-out spray.

You heard about this guy in Bangkok who . . .
Oh God, this chick is going to murder you . . .
your name . . . *The New York Post* . . . *'Indomitable'*
*Superspy Neutralized in Stupid Way* . . .
soon as your stiff is sniffed out you'll get canned . . .
still, everybody's gotta go someday . . .
besides, she's pretty (sort of) . . . dimples . . . and . . .

Masseuse and chair dissolve. You tumble under
but plummet upward through a fog, forgetting
Newton's laws. The dream at first is free
of frame, content and continuity,
so, when the cloudscape scatters and a setting
fades into focus, you can only wonder…

How did you get to Pitt and Rivington?
On foot? By bus? And what's this sense of loss?
Recent bereavement? Failure to have won?
Yes, and the tug of what you should have done
but didn't. Trauma you should tell the boss
with great strain breaks the surface: *You were caught;*
*the box is lost forever.*
                          You should call,
but not before you grab a beer and chill.
Besides, this hood is heaven: whiffs of pot,
hipsters in headphones, hoochies shod to kill,
tattoos, graffiti tags, and, best of all,
beaucoup cantinas. Feels like happy hour.

ID in hand, you're next in line to enter
a cheapie called the Down-And-Out Café
when Chinatown erupts: a gamma ray
geysers as high as the Verizon tower,
green cloud swirls about an epicenter,
and sultry winds are liquefying blocks
of stoops and stonework, garbage cans, crosswalks.

*Some moron must have cracked that effing box.*

Brick drips like coffee. Traffic signals droop
their heavy heads, and molten roads like soup
absorb them. Feel that? Fuel tanks are blowing—
a Maserati, a delivery van,
a flatbed sinking in the act of towing
a Beamer. Thirty yards out vintage stores,
spas, and cafés are caving in, the floors
above them sagging, plopping down.
                                    Oh man,
tonight you party with the dinosaurs.
No need to bother dialing nine-one-one.
Hello, extinction. You don't even run,
just founder in your mucky soles and stare.
A great wave crashes. Then you aren't there.

. . . Pitches . . . staccato . . . quavering the way
rounds from an automatic ricochet
off metal siding. Ah yes—Mandarin.
The Dragon's Claw, the T'ang, the Righteous Fists
rush back as reasons for the bind you're in:
a shipping office, fastened to a chair.
The brimstone blistering your calves and wrists
is only duct tape tugging at your hair.
Stop straining, idiot.
                              The caterwaul
is emanating from an Asian guy
armed with Armani and a paisley tie.
He's shouting orders at a cell, his stare
fixed on abstraction. When he ends the call,
knock, knock, *jinlai!*, and another dude
comes in—grotesquely muscled, neck-tattooed,
tough as a thug can look who's five feet tall.
He bows and hands the suit a burlap sack.

What's in it? Torture tools? A brick of smack?
No, there's a hum, a far from soothing drone
barbed like a hive, charged as a power station,
broadcasting bad vibrations through the floor.
Must be the Claw, but harsher than before,
as though its contents hungered to be known.

When Bossman peeks inside the bag, a geyser
of phosphorescent gamma radiation
erupts and rakes his features from beneath.
Martians are dancing on his cheeks, his eyes are

Hubble pics of quasars, and his teeth
sheep from Chernobyl. Dude looks freaking nuts,
like Mr. Yuk, like evil.
                    When he's done,
he sends the goon out with the sideshow, shuts
the door, and cracks his knuckles, one by one.
Looks like it's torture time. You know the drill:
the leather glove, the simper, the cheesecake
Gestapo glare that swears *my iron vill*
*vill pinch you, sqveeze you, crush you till you break.*

He slaps you some to make sure you're awake
then starts in:
                    "Say our worker movement seem
no-work fantastic plan—you big mistake:
we conquer global-wide. We mighty dream.
Like little cinder kindle prairie fire,
baby explosion no more New York City.

I Chairman of American Committee
here under hero mission to acquire
People esteem back from obese, bourgeois,
white devil Uncle Sam. This mighty day
come box, but what inside? Informant say
you big imperialist poodle, so
be true like Boy Scout or I shoot you slow:
what kind disease or bomb in Dragon Craw?"

You stare him down awhile before replying,
with perfect candor,
                    "I don't fucking know."

Yep, here it comes—a wallop on the jaw
takes you to school. Spittle and teeth go flying.
Your vision reels, but what was that you saw
beside the trashcan in the corner, lying
atop some bubble wrap? A red box cutter,
the razor jutting from its dimpled grip.

This time when Himmler asks about the Craw
you treat him to a double round of lip:

"You deaf or somethin', dick-face? Did I stutter?"

He winds his fist up farther than before.
*T-minus three, two, one—Kapow!* You tip
over. The chair escorts you to the floor.
Shamming a fit, you kick and wriggle, scrape
closer and closer, just a little more . . .
*there.*
         With a square toe battering your abs,
you go to work. It's clumsy—bits of tape,
slivers of wrist, but, once your hands escape,
they're all about revenge: the left one grabs
the loafer in your stomach, while the right
hacks his Achilles tendon. Down he goes.
The razor finds the windpipe, and the fight
is draining from him, spurting through the slit.
The spasms flatline, but the eyes don't close.

Your insides mist when death is intimate.

Back in the cruel world, what a mess:
blood from his gizzard, from your wrists, the sockets

where molars used to live. The ugliness
of what you gift and get.
                              His jacket pockets
cough up a Quad-band cell, a ring of keys,
a Sig Sauer, and a nine-mil magazine;
his pants, a wallet crammed with sham IDs,
platinum cards, and snapshots of a son
decked out as G.I. Joe for Halloween.
The kid is cute.
                              Only a psychopath
could chuckle looking at the families.
How many sons and dear ol' dads you done?
Gazillions—now's no time to work the math.
Suck it up, killer. Grab the stupid gun;
assassinate compassion. Once you've won,
you can repent and wimp out of the Bureau.
It's not too late to be a children's hero,
a clown that bends balloons, the Lord of Fun.

One mean squint,
                    you scan a hallway
void of goons
                and video surveillance.
Through the threshold next door,
                        thick sound thumping.
You ease an ear up
                outside the frame:
*Queen*'s "Rhapsody,"
                and you can't help catching
what sounds like sex
                synchronized to the beat.
A tad turned on,
                you twist and steal
a hardcore peep
                at (surprise) not porn:

gloved and grunting,
                girt with a weight belt,
the punk you saw,
                the pygmy, is pumping
big-ass barbells,
                his back toward you,
that sack beside him.

                You stalk him softly,
but the floor is foam.
                He feels footsteps,
groans *Who . . . dat?*
              Your gun-butt greets him
hard on the head.

                    Hundred pounders
mash the mat;
                    the man drops after.
You bolt with the bag then,
                    the box inside it
welcome weight.


                    In the warehouse, walls
bricked with crates
                    and cardboard cartons
barricade your flanks.
                    Born to pry,
you slide a lid off,
                    sift through strata
of gangland capital:
                    coffee, coca,
and dragon dust,
                    dandruff of dreams.
The Maoists' main line
                    to American life.


Round a forklift, past
                    a pillar of pallets,
you stumble on someone
                    sitting, stiff-backed,
in a folding chair:
                    a chick, Chinese,
bound and gagged.
                    Babes are drags,
last thing you need's
                    another nuisance,
but her damn doe-eyes
                    have done you in.

Ropes razored,
                        she rips tape off
her scrunched kisser,
                        and the screech that escapes her
scratches silence.
                        So much for subtlety!
You yank hard,
                        and she yelps but yields,
comes with cussing.


                        Crimson letters
light an *EXIT*,
                        and you lunge for them, lugging
both the relic
                        and your bonus baggage—
Tag-along Sue.
                        The telltale tramp
of goons approaching,
                        you punch the push bar
and find Chinatown
                        chock-full and chafing.
A mob immerses you:
                        mothers shoving
strollers, shopkeepers
                        stacking street side
produce displays.
                        You part the sea
with oaths and elbows.
                        Over your shoulder
the whole hooligan
                        horde emerges,
shouting and shooting.
                        *Shit, shit, and shit!*—

the chick in heels,

        the chest heavy,

and the gangsters gaining.

           You get creative,

slip up a side street,

          but it swerves and tapers,

turns out blind—

        brick walls, backdoors

locked and barred.

        On lines above you

panties and push-ups,

          private choices,

work it in earthly

        urban air.

No ladder, though,

        no ledge to leap for.


At your feet, a plate

        framed by flagstones.

It's loose, and you lift it,

        let light in:

six feet down,

      a sewer sighs

the ordure of the day.

        The damn damsel

flails and coughs up

       fierce *Fuck-no*s,

but, crap, what other

        option *is* there?

"Pick it, princess:

        poo-water or them."

In old Manhattan the comptrolling wisdom
of Tammany embezzlers did decree
storm drains and sewage pipes would run together
right underneath the street. This rip-off system
has always backed up during crappy weather
and flushed unfiltered offal out to sea.

Although it last rained several days ago,
the works are still knee-high in overflow,
and you, all nose, are savoring a rank
aroma—*eau du ruptured septic tank.*
Darkness intensifies the fragrance, dank
darkness. You only know the girl's in tow
because the poor thing keeps on getting sick,
Vesuvially, inches from your back.

You grope, grope, grope the relic from the sack,
and foxfire feeds your squint a vaulted brick
cradle and life that makes you miss the dark:
a winged snake straight out of *Jurassic Park,*
a gilled rat brandishing a caudal fin,
mouse-headed mollusks, and a two-faced toad
whose five eyes severally take you in.

God, what a freak show! Optic overload.
The damsel lapses into wild behavior,
sometimes mounting you, her chair, her savior,
to keep the creeps from nibbling her toes,
sometimes withdrawing to an Arctic distance
in passionate denial of your existence.

Come-ons, rebuffs, embraces, separations—
God, what a schizo! Round and round she goes.

You reach out, try to normalize relations.
After a "hey there," conversation flows:
her name's Li-ling, and she can call you Bob;
she holds degrees, you slave at menial tasks
of no account. All's cool until she asks
why you were visiting the Chinese mob.
You crack your cover blabbing:
                                                        "Gotta get
this package safely to the Feds—that's it.
For stiffs like me, you know, a job's a job."

She halts mid-slosh and trumpets in a huff:

"I know what that box is—the Dragon's Claw!
The legend's true, I mean, the thing is glowing.
Just think of all the nasty evil stuff
fermenting in there for millennia.
You—you're just going to give it up not knowing
what the government will use it for?
Um, weapons research? Next-wave tools of war?
Are you a cyborg drone or just naïve?
What adult brain could actually believe
'protect and serve' and all that 'hoo-rah' nonsense
the D.O.D. calls glory? Sorry, 'dude,'
duty does not excuse a lack of conscience."

Well, she can talk, but where's the gratitude?
You know her caste—those namaste, wheatgrass,
free-love-forever snobs that live to spout

slander against corn syrup, the devout,
oil rigs, the military, blah, blah, blah,
like loving one's own country's lower class.

"Yeah, I'm a drone, the drone that saved your ass."

She only grows more strident:
                                "You no doubt
are unaware the legend of the Claw
prescribes a cure—a Phoenix statuette
pumped full of antidote to neutralize
that vat of venom there. Well, check this out:
today, when I was working at the Met
(where I curate a world-class collection),
a faience Phoenix lights up, like, 'Surprise!,'
dead center of the First Imperial section.
Before I reached it, though, those gangster guys
grabbed me and gave me this insane pop quiz
about that chest you're holding, what it is
and why it vibrates.
                                Listen, here's the deal:
because the box is 'on,' the threat is real,
and we should use my Phoenix to defang
that cataclysm there before the T'ang,
the Pentagon, or, worse yet, Quantico
co-opts its powers. Once the oomph is gone,
you're free to find your boss and run a con,
hand him, you know, a dud instead.
                                But, Oh,
when those shlemiels were grilling me this morning,
I kind of told them (maybe it was dumb),
about the figurine, I mean, so, um,

they may be waiting at the Met. Fair warning.
If things get nasty . . . well, we'll wait and see.
So long as we can screw the perps in power,
it's worth it. Trust me. I'm a PhD."

This chick embodies all your baldest fears.
Though you have known her only half an hour,
the hurt's like you've been married forty years—
no warmth, no nookie, just a vice-like will
mashing your manliness.
                              Your plans are still
unreconciled when something tall appears
just up the tunnel—humanoid in shape,
sporting a mustache and magician's cape.
Its gaping arms suggest a hug; its eyes
portals to revelation or psychosis.

*Who is this jackass? Death? The modern Moses?*
*Charles Manson in a Dracula disguise?*
*Your day so far has been one long, bizarre*
*B-movie, so why not this wacko, too?*

When he intones,
                    "we've been expecting you,"
you mutter,
                    "well, I guess, like, here we are."

# Part III: The One True Religion

In Qinghai Province modest dunes entomb
Emperor Zhuanxu and a reading room
where you might find, among the spooled remains
of handscrolls from a literary age,
quaint metaphysics by a nameless sage.

*The Dragon and the Phoenix,* he maintains,
*are Fire-fathered twins, and Time, their mother,*
*rouses them every hundred thousand years*
*to feud until they neutralize each other.*

The guy is really good on how it's done:

*. . . just after dawn, a lizard grimace rears*
*out of a crater, scratches gouge the edges,*
*and bat-wings flex their webbing in the sun.*
*Earth shudders meanwhile, and a ripe divide*
*discharges fowl that in an instant fledges,*
*leans leeward, and remembers how to glide.*

*Drawn, then, by more than mating magnetism*
*each toward its bane, they intertwine and fight*
*like yin and yang, the darkness and the light,*
*because they must: since the original schism*
*wedded warfare to the way of things,*
*tension alone can keep the world in balance.*

*Red shrieks incendiary, claws and talons*
*tattering feather-clad and leathern wings,*
*they rage straight through to twilight in the air, in*

the crater lakes their combat slaps and churns
and over acreage their breath makes barren.
He-thunderbird, she-wyrm, they take their turns
winning and losing, till climactic spasms
sunder them, and daylight disappears,
and they collapse into adjacent chasms
to sleep another hundred thousand years.

The Coleman swinging from the mole man's hand
will do for lighting, so you stow the chest.
(The golden rule of tradecraft: contraband
is happiest withheld from public view.)

Limbs rigid in attention, fingers pressed
against his brow, the freak addresses you
like you're Director of Starfleet Command
or something:
       "Convert phase progressed as planned.
I preached your coming, and the faithful few
are settled comfortably in their quarters,
training, praying, and awaiting orders."

That snapped, he bows, then ushers you through older
construction, archways, vaulted intersections,
a local yokel following directions
long since instinctual. The city's dregs
are cresting past your knees. Your feet get colder.
Septic slitherers caress your legs.
Winged vermin tease your hair. The damsel cracks
and freaks again but, when you squeeze her shoulder
and murmur,
       "Take a pill, man, chill, relax,"
she screeches,
       "Keep your skeezy paws off me,
you redneck pervert,"
       so you leave her be.

After an hour negotiating slick
avenues of primordial goo, your guide
stops sloshing, slaps the tunnel's out-curved side
and climbs a service ladder. Though the chick
is giddier than you to leave the realm
of muck, methane, and mythic alligators,
you yank her down and mount the rungs above her.

Head poking through a hatchway, you discover
an age-old pumping house, forgotten helm
of what was once a hands-on operation.
Among the vats and flow-gauge regulators,
more recent signs of human habitation
reveal themselves: a Maglite, cooking fires,
patio chairs, a cardboard bathroom stall.
Snug little caskets populate a wall
like catacombs, and fishnets tied to wires
resemble hammocks on a whaling ship.

Bodies are in them, but asleep, not dead.

A funny sort of plumbing, *drip, drip, drip,*
leaks from the spalling concrete overhead.
The vibe is chill, the scattered snoring slow,
tranquil, and then your tour guide trumpets:
                                        "Lo!
The savior has arrived! Arise! Arise!"

And they are tumbling from bunks and slings
and lurching toward you—troglodytes with dirt
for skin, sporadic teeth, and vermin eyes

stretching your t-shirt, tugging at her skirt,
groping you, groping you, your private things.
Will the psychotics running through your pockets
go on to rip your limbs out of their sockets?
Those maws—will they devour not just you,
but sweet Li-ling, your little pit bull, too?

Sensing the ticklishness of your position,
their keeper scolds,

           "Down, brethren! More respect.
That one not only is a higher power
sent from the stars to shepherd the elect,
he is our guest."

            Tsk-tsked into submission,
aspiring cannibals disperse and cower,
hangdog, in corners of the fire-lit cell.
Still short of breath, you sputter,

            "What the hell?
What is this sideshow, *Cro-mags Jacked On Crack*?"

He beams:

         "Ingenious! More than worldly wise!
Casting aspersions on our origins
so that we prove our faith. Well, well! Sit back
and hear the Testament of How-I-Woke-
to-Knowledge-of-the-Astral-Enterprise."

Attendant crazies shamble through the smoke
dragging a pair of plastic storage bins.
You and the doctor sit, and he begins:

"It's true: before the Cosmic Spirit spoke
salvation through me, and I earned the name
Elijah Five, I was a waste of shame—
the late-night freak who whoops before he thinks
and only asks, *Why not? Why not more drinks?*

*Why not a snort? Some smack? Why not? I'll take it,*
until he's washed up, squatting on the street.

In fact, the night God found me I was naked
atop a picnic bench in Central Park,
waiting for White Cross Kaksonjae to spark
Gomorrah in my head. It was the heat,
you see, that made me strip, a dense, moist, gritty
misery, and the wind refused to blow.
A surge had crashed the grid and dimmed the city.
The stars for once were putting on a show.

Then came the rush. Believe you me, I know
hallucinations, what a scam they are.
This vision was a wholly different deal.
A laser shot out of the Morning Star
and smote my godless brain, the blast so real
that doubt went steaming downwind out my eyes,
and echoes in my skull commanded:
                                        *Rise,*
*lost soul, and learn the reason you are here*
*on earth and in the skin you wear. One year*
*you are to roam the land they call Manhattan,*
*preaching the coming of a global terror*
*and Him-Who-Holds-The-Cure, the boon, the bearer*
*of many titles: Lucifer in Latin,*
*Haleel in Hebrew, Phosphoros in Greek.*
*After this term illuminating humans,*
*anoint your most devoted catechumens*
*and lead them underground to wait and pray.*
*What year, what month, what date I cannot say,*

*but you shall know the champion you seek*
*by certain signs. Be grateful, now, and do*
*the work that you must do.*
                          The beam withdrew,
and morning broke, and from that hour the sun
like bleach has scorched my eyes. I preached at night
in Herald Square and, when the term was done,
packed up and shepherded my faithful few
outside the world to wait for you, the one
the stars foretold, the bringer of the light.
Share, now, the miracle!"
                          The cockroach men
are getting restless, skittering again.
There's no escape, no other way to work it—
you yank the relic out, and emerald green
appeasement storms the cell. A sacred circuit
marries off the seeing and the seen.
For years these freaks were waiting for a sign,
and now it's in your hands, absurd, divine,
insisting, *Yes, my children, the outrageous*
*nonsense you worship happens to be true.*

You start to smirk, but fervor is contagious.
These wackos found their truth, and who are you
to mock it? Why dismiss a grand design
that makes you Messianic middleman?
Faith is a nice, warm place. You like the feel
and have already half-succumbed to zeal,
when Li-ling whispers,
                          "Alright, here's the plan:
because these lepers think you're, like, for real,

play along, preach like Jesus or whatever,
till we escape their thrice-most-holy sewer."

You can't help starting to respect her—clever
at strategy, more deviant than you are.
Hells yeah!, why not assume the deity
everyone won't stop nagging you to be?

Yeah! Because God is what the people want,
you heft the light aloft and shake it, flaunt
your awesomeness. And when you beat the drum,
you boom like James Earl Jones, the King, the Boss,
hopped up on glory, tolling gravitas:

"High Priests of What-It-Is-That-Soon-Must-Come,
you prayed a sacred signal would appear,
and, Lo!, I leapt the parsecs and am here,
the astral answer humming in my hands.
Now, since the What-We-All-Adore demands
not just belief and daily discipline,
but action, I must ask you: can you men
breathe fire? Can you laugh at death and doubt?"

Gruff affirmation, with a cough mixed in,
bounces around the concrete cell.
                                        "Come, then,
lead me in glory, by a covert route,
north to your Met Museum to install
this relic in a temple. Heathen thieves
may well be there to frustrate us with all
the naughtiness the godless can contrive,
but we shall prove an army that believes
fears nothing, Yea, fears nothing. Look alive,
now, brethren. We depart at once."
                                        The cheer
that storms your senses bristles with conviction,
the mindless kind that muddies fact with fiction
and only takes in what it wants to hear,

but Oh! how grand the sound is! Off you go,
you and your crazed crusaders, with dispatch
dropping like paratroopers down the hatch
into the outhouse atmosphere below.

During the ninety-block excursion north,
you bark harangues and swagger back and forth
among the Knights of the Celestial Box
to learn their names and how their brains were fried:
there's "Ponzi" Pete who lost his wife in stocks
and picked religion over suicide;
Ju-Jack the mime that endless acid trips
cracked into five personas; Ted the dentist,
disbarred for "huffing gas and peddling scrips;"
some ogre known as "Hook" who had apprenticed
in carpentry until he lost a hand;
and dozens more, each with a tragic story,
and all committed to the greater glory
of nonsense only God could understand.

Li-ling, thank God, is silent at your side,
observing, smirking, more than satisfied
now that you're doing what she said was best,
and all the while the pressure builds—the chest
pulses and thrums as if the cryptic forces
jailed an age within its jade were giddy
to storm creation.
                    So by zigzag courses
you navigate the slop of New York City
until the soldiers in the vanguard stop
sloshing and stand beside a service shaft.
A ladder leads to darkness. There's a draft.

You stub your fingers bumping at the top—
metal, a manhole cover, upper boundary
of Trogland proper.
                          Funny that, of all
the public works you've visited today,
your mind should pick this moment to replay
scenes from an exposé about the foundry
that casts Manhattan's iron: *West Bengal.*
*Sticks without shirts or health insurance tilting*
*all hell into a mold. A slip-up wilting*
*the total market value of a limb.*
*Each shift roulette on a volcano's rim.*
You're gonna need hot luck, chutzpah, and hustle
to get your dodgy job done, same as them.

Hooking your legs inside the rungs, you muscle
the cover off. The scrape is loud. The night
recoils, calms, and breathes like three a.m.
*All's well.* The box tucked safely out of sight,
you ease your devotees out of the Valley
of Noxious Fumes into the upper air.
*All's well, all's well,* and then headlights ignite
and hold you focal in their leveled glare.
Orders are shouted, engines kicked awake,
and, *Whoa!,* a whole damn motorcycle rally
revs as one and roars out of the alley.

*Damn commies are impossible to shake!*
Your instincts zero in and spin about
the million-dollar question: should you break
north for the Met or stand and fight it out?

Fuck it, fight:

    it's fate or something.
Hoo-ah!, you square off,

     squint and squeeze,
but the sodden Sig

    spites you, spits up
muzzle fizzle.

    Your euphoria fades
when rounds rake

     your parade in answer:
Blaise the Haitian

    with braids down his back,
"Mad-dog" Marty—

     martyred, blasted
beyond belief.


    As you leap with Li-ling
behind a pair

    of post office boxes,
your dazed crusaders

     duck behind dumpsters
and hunker down.

    The heathen horde
circles, assesses.

    A siege commences.
Frantic to defend

    front and flanks,
your grunts grab garbage

     and go ballistic:
bottles are shells,

    and shards, shrapnel;

soggy bottoms
                        of brown paper bags
explode on helmets,
                        their payloads poison,
like napalm or nerve gas,
                        but not enough—
a couple of goons
                        recoil and crash;
the rest rally.

                        Rounds keep winging
your trash artillerists
                        until, click, click,
the storm subsides.
                        Stirred by the lull,
your devotees slam
                        the dumpsters shut,
leap on the lids,
                        and launch their rage
headlong at the onslaught,
                        unhorsing the hoodlums.
Bodies are rolling;
                        riderless road bikes
slumping sideways.

                        Still not enough:
the fallen goons
                        flip to their feet
and strike up stances,
                        the Snake, the Dragon.
(Dudes got degrees,
                        dojo doctorates
in the chops of the master,

                         Charlie Chan.)
Crude in contrast,
                    your psychotic cavemen
blitz like zombies,
                    berserkers zealous
to kill and be killed.
                         The clash is ageless:
formal perfection,
                    free-style frenzy—
which school will pack
                         more punch in practice?
You eye the melee
                    a moment, admiring
the epicness of it,
                    then enter the fray
on the side of the mad.


                         A slow-mo, celluloid
fight-scene spools
                    in front of your fists:
jaws are popped,
                    and a pug nose pancaked;
kicks reduced
                    to compound fractures;
bad blood let.
                    Better yet,
the prof gets down
                    and dirty, dredges
a two-by-four toothed
                    with twisted nails
from a construction bin
                    and strikes with strength
you never imagined

                   muscles could muster.
Pent-up repugnance
               exploding, seeking
freedom through carnage,
                   her cries are cracked,
her triumph total.
             You two alone
are still standing
             when sirens signal
*Cops are coming!*

            You collar Xena
the Warrior Princess
              and pull her past
a circle of stiffs,
            at the center of which
lies Elijah,
          the leal believer,
to whom the bright
             box you are bearing
meant so much.
          Mighty the man
who fights for a faith,
            false or true.

You and Cruella take a tree-lined trail
at jailbreak speeds until you shake the wail
of pork collecting round the battle-scene.
Because the groves and shrubberies that screen
Frederick Olmstead's monumental lawn
are late-night sanctuary from the law,
you meet, in passing, knots of derelicts:
freebasers bleeding from a recent fix,
a squeaky shemale and her Wall Street john
mid-ooh-la-la, and bums, a wind quintet,
snoring around an empty bottle. *Ah,*
*New York, New York at night.*
                    Just as the Met
emerges from the elms, the Dragon's Claw
horse-kicks your grip, as if millennia
of caged rampage had cracked and rammed the lid.
The temper tantrum looses shockwaves; sparks
precipitate from streetlights, lightning arcs
from post to post. A flash, then, and the grid
has crashed, and you are hunkered on your knees,
Li-ling secure between your chest and arms.

It's just the stars now, shedding through the trees
a phantom light that makes you think of farms,
backwater acres in an unplugged past.
Funny, you kinda oughta thank that blast
for blacking all things out this side of Park—
no video surveillance, no alarms.

It's like the neighborhood, by going dark,
is saying *sin at will; you won't get caught.*

You glide by grey cube trucks and loading docks
on feline feet that stiffen when you spot
a zippo lighting up a watchman's box:
some total tool is trying to repair
the obvious lack of power everywhere
by tap-tap-tapping on an empty screen.

You tell the PhD to lure him out
by putting on a 'poor lost lamb' routine.
After a few hair-flips and snorts of doubt,
she proves a perfect ham, her nasal pleas
pure pathos. When he runs to help, you trap
his throat inside your elbow, flex and squeeze
until his legs quit thrashing. (Sorry sap
works graveyard—he should thank you for the nap.)

After some endless fumbling with the keys,
she tugs you through a hall to galleries
jam-packed with eyes, cats, crowns, room after room
of keepsakes plundered from some pickled pharaoh.
No harm, no foul till, fumbling through a narrow
passage that serves the reconstructed tomb,
you ding your funny bone on something hard.
Your *Fuck!* echoes, and what would be a guard
from round a corner bounces a command
to "Freeze, dirt-bag! Surrender!"
                                        *Doh, you're made.*

You hand your date the swaddled contraband
and whisper,
                    "Prep the relics—you're the prof."

With that, you bellow, charge, and carom off
a fleshy mass that swivels and pursues you
through the Great Hall, up the Grand Cascade,
into the Art of Europe.
                                    Dude who laid
this dump out did his damnedest to confuse you—
halls feeding halls, all more or less the same.
Worse, circle, jump, or juke, you just can't burn
the bastard. Rhino's got a running game.

Around a bend in Holland, you discern
moonlight through windows and a moonlit slick
along the floor, the leavings of a mop.
Shameful, but there it is—the oldest trick.

You bait the trap with taunts,
                                    "Yoo-hoo! Come quick!
I'm gonna spray-paint *Donald Trump's A Creep*
on Rembrandt's *Jesus*!"
                                    When the rent-a-cop
runs in, he runs in place, his feet a blur
until they both fly up. His coccyx-flop
thuds through the halls. While squeezing him to sleep,
you murmur mercifully, like you were
a bushman begging pardon from his prey:

"So sorry. There was just no other way."

Another chess-piece taken out of play,
you backtrack, panting, to the landing where
you first decided to resist arrest.
No question where the doctor schlepped the chest:
off to your left a mystic laser show
is beaconing you through the dusty air.
No time to take a breather, off you go
to gut the beast and end this whole affair.

Tracking the dazzle through the Asian wing
past dimpled Buddhas, landscape scrolls, a herd
of elephants, a tribe of randy scholars,
you reach the triptych you desire—Li-ling
setting a sharp-beaked little Firebird
beside the Dragon's Claw, both relics blurred
by their own glare. It's time to end this thing
and drain an eighth of triumph.
                                When she hollers
"Now!" above the molar-rattling buzz,
you draw the red box-cutter, flick the blade,
and pry the ancient lock out of the jade.
The lid leaps open. Phosphorescent green
evil invades the hall and, as it does,
the doctor drops the Phoenix figurine.

You've seen two Tesla coils with lightning lashes
smiting each other's crowns, and psychedelic
strobes at a discothèque, ecstatic flashes
piercing your eyes and bouncing round your skull—
that's how the fight looks, relic zapping relic,
until *Ka-boom!* like the sensational
finale of a pyrotechnics show,
like Chinese New Year: comets, whirlies—whoa! . . .

Once the kaleidoscopic aftershocks
have scattered from your vision, and the room
settles again into its off-hour gloom,
the Dragon's Claw looks like a carved jade box;

the Phoenix like the wreck of what was art.
The day you just survived would seem, from start
to finish, total fiction, genre nonsense,
except she's there, your prof, your proof, your conscience,
eying you with approval. You're a hero.
You should be knighted for your victory.
The Dragon has been smited, and the Bureau
need never know you blasted all the fun
out of its precious weapon: *Golly gee,
I found it dead like this—not even one
old virus, not a single megaton.*

You did the right thing, crazy-ass but prudent,
and now feel like your spying days are done.
High time to shuck disguises, drown the gun,
and play, no, *be* the student, just a student,
don the gown and mount the stage next year
with pomp, circumstance, and a Two Point Oh.
Then sharper duds, a less absurd career,
and marriage to some chick like . . . *Jesus, No!*
The dream seizes before your dude-most fear.

As Li-ling leads you out of the Museum,
you keep your distance, feeling it would be, um,
unsafe to walk too close. She's hot and all,
but Harvard types like her get off on rules
and no-nos. Even her behind looks bossy.
Blink, and she'd make your life a lecture hall,
her friends exams. You hear them now: a posse
of vegan ivy-leaguers, total tools,
exchanging painfully grammatical

lampoons of you as a Neanderthal
behind your back. Why bother? With her brains,
not all your smarm could coax her into drinking
two-for-one *Jäger* bombs and surfing trains.

Come on, moron, you just saved the city,
the whole world, maybe. What you doing thinking
about a girlfriend? You are in your prime.
Go lay whatever's more than halfway pretty.
As for the lifemate crap, there will be time.

Your deluxe taxi
                 took the Transverse
and has swung, squealing,
                       south toward the Village.
A lounge lizard
               loving the velour,
you rest easy,
                relic to your right,
to your left, Li-ling.
                   Your leg and hers,
with each rev and curve,
                   keep percussing,
grinding even.
               Goddamn girl-crazy,
you're spy enough
                   to know never
bring babe-baggage
                 on Bureau business.

When you grab the goods
                     and get out, set on
strolling, solo,
               to the southside dead-drop,
she reacts fast.
               Before you can feed her
something pat
               like *See ya, sweetheart,*
*thanks for the thrills,*
                 she throws open
the door opposite
               and pre-empts your exit

with a sharp, "Shut up.

We're sharing this."

You're too damn pooped

to preach protocol,
run her off,

or rub her out.
Besides, her scowl

scares you, so…

you lead her up Leroy,

low-rent home
to a blasé box

of brickwork primed
a smog-like gray.

Spalling stencils
proclaim *Ma Hava's*

*Wholesale Challah.*
That's Warehouse Delta.

Midway up the wall,
a little late-night

delivery window,
bottom-hinged

with a barrel-bolt hasp.
A simple set-up,

secret only
because who questions

the commonplace?

Soon as you've slid

the spent box in,
swung the door up

and drawn the deadbolt,

a low-watt light bulb
                          left of the frame
glows green—that means
                                you're golden: goldarn
commies failed;
                      freedom prevailed.
Whoo-hah! a win.
                          Welp, though absent
spliffs and Schlitz
                        to celebrate success with,
you've got a girl.


                      Gaze evasive,
she eyes asphalt
                      and air a while,
then laughs, leans in
                          and lets you have it:

"My bet is, 'Bob,'
                          your business requires
phone books full
                        of fake ids.
Which do you wear
                          when the workday's done?"


"Zach Berzinski."


                      "Gesundheit, Polack."


Cellar plundered,
                        sunken secrets
up in the open,
                        your options dwindle

to termination
                    or total trust.

A funny feeling
                    forces your hand
to guide the crisis
                    across the carless
West Side Highway.
                    The Hudson is handsome;
Jersey City
                    not so unsightly
at night. It's pleasant.
                    The pageant puts out
the required romance:
                    if the Colgate Clock
harks back to hygiene
                    in homes where hearts were,
Goldman Sachs'
                    skyscraper stands
for futures and fortunes,
                    failures, maybe,
and the moon's mood lighting
                    has made a milieu
where even those Ur-
                    arch-enemies,
the famed Dragon
                    and Phoenix, might defy
their rival natures,
                    nest, and nuzzle.

Close your eyes—
                    the kiss has come.

# Part IV: Good Morning, Twilight

Sorry to butt in while you're making out
with Ms. Levine, but there's a second myth
that's out there spoiling to be reckoned with.
Believe in it, believe the Greater Doubt
was born American and not so long ago:

July the 2nd, 1947.
Fords motored, Hoovers hooved, and Joltin' Joe
twice fed the cheap seats homers. All was well,
we said our prayers, and *Whoa*—just past eleven
a ghostly hubcap off some wheel of heaven
streaked the dark and struck New Mexico.

When call-in shows lit up with *What the Hell?*,
official mouths were on the air repeating
*no warhead, just a storm balloon that fell*
*on cattleland. The so-called 'eerie glow'*
*was Roswell bouncing off reflective sheeting*
*Roswell to Roswell.*
                              While we heard, we jeered
*Horsefeathers! Hogwash! Hooey!* We had fallen
for fudge before. No more. The fiends we feared
demanded horrors:
                              dads were gruffly certain
that gremlin at the Kremlin, Joseph Stalin,
had up and chucked some Nazi-engineered
surveillance disc over the Iron Curtain
to give our wives and drive-ins dirty looks,

and four-eyed dorkwads high on comic books
tormented malt shops with the weirdo thesis—
*Golly Gee, the way the thing was spinning,*
*it only could have dropped from outer space.*
*This contact clearly beacons the beginning*
*of probes, death-rays, and bye-bye human race.*

When Covert Ops ransacked the scrub for pieces
to truck by night to Edwards Air Force Base,
what wreckage nestled in a cactus bed
escaped the sweep?
                        Arms, guts, a hunk of head,
out there for decades, restless to reveal
life that will make us slaves
                            or stuff mass graves
until we learn to praise its post-human ideal.

Fresh pillow and a bed not yours, but deeper.
What stranger-flesh is there? What corpse or sleeper?

You mash your lids in search of who and where,
and Holy . . . *you and Harvard tongued at dawn,*
*fogged up a taxi heading to her place,*
*and nodded off before you got it on.*

Check out your paramour, how far the hair
has bubbled up above her planted face;
look how her tuckus juts into the air:
Li-ling Levine, the Doc, in tanga panties.
(Though not quite the marriage of true minds,
you made a wicked pair of vigilantes.)

What must be twilight purpling the blinds
says Physics cycled past like you were dead.
Another midterm missed, a last chance blown.
Dude, you're a loser once you leave this bed.
Besides, her figure is . . .
     A saxophone
awoogas from the hardwood where your jeans
are wadded. *Peter Gunn* the ringtone means
Bureau Director Uh-Oh One is calling
to squawk *Wake up, wake up, the sky is falling!*
*You go catch it.* Coot has got the power
to drain your savings, so there's no real choice.
You tap *Accept.*
     A wet Kentucky cough

typhoons your earpiece. While he roots for voice,
you whimper:
            "Come on, boss, a few days off . . .
furlough till sunup . . . midnight . . . half an hour?"

"Vacation! Killer, that's for nine-to-fivers.
Our roster took some hits, and you survivors
gonna shuck your nine lives overtime.
Anyways, didn't you *get off* last night? . . .
Miss Twiggy? . . . Oh, now, no one dropped a dime.
I watched you swapping spit by satellite.
Yeah, yeah, how creepy, what a perv I am,
but let's get down to saving Uncle Sam:

while filtering through fresh domestic chatter
for dirt on *Los Banditos* drug cartel,
the boys in Desert West Surveillance caught
this random jackass yacking on his cell
about some space-age trillion-gigawatt
thing-a-ma-jigger. (What it *does* don't matter.)
Sucker sang he 'ganked' it from the sand
outside Who-Gives-A-Rip, New Mexico.

The next J. Edgar Hoover he is not—
Facebook has tagged him playing in a band
(*Mimosa*, no, *Miasma*, yeah, that's right),
and there's our prize dead-center in the show.
Now, since *Mimosa*'s booked a gig tonight
at Bowery Ballroom, shower off and go
collect my tech-toy. There's your need-to-know.
You're welcome.
            Dammit, though, the Bureau's got a
nasty infestation: rats and moles.

Stinks but, as yet, I've dug up bupkis, nada,
not even droppings round old hidey holes.
So, till the nest is torched, we improvise.
From here out run a passkey shibboleth,
you know, like ball teams back in World War II,
to tell the suspect many from the few
true joes we trust. This joke is life or death:

The windup—*Why do pigs make perfect spies?*

The dinger—*'Cause they're always in-hog-nito.*

Haw, Haw! You get it?
                              Alright, lady-killer,
shore leave is over. Shove your freak libido
back in your pants, praise God, and get to work.
And if, you know, this grab-n-go turns thriller,
no mercy. Yours is not to wonder why.
Just do or die, li'l buddy, do or die."

The line goes dead, and you are left to wonder
why you adore an alcoholic jerk.
Childhood abuse? Meatheads that called you sissy?
You grew to love the distant intimacy
that couples grunt to sergeant, spy to spy.
As for the other sex, you kind of blunder
from bed to bed and vanish when they cry.

So, Sleeping Beauty—should you say goodbye?
Nah, leave her dormant; slip a Hallmark under
her Android there. You commandeer a pen,
rip off a strip of scratch, and carve in crude
block letters:

*Fun last night but, sorry, dude,*
*I gotta go and save the world again.*
*Call me if you are ever in the mood.*
*That's all.*
(A number stands in for your name.)

The safer style's Siberia, since warm
words, when you risk them, always come off lame.
The sniper rifles hoarded in your dorm,
objectives, tradecraft, and a tranquil aim
in times of crisis—these are things you know.

The cozier she looks, the more it's time to go.

A power walk across the patchwork quilt,
and here you are, a few blocks east of fancy,
your All Stars scuffing that Manhattan silt,
your pupils grooving on the signs and symbols
dusk ignites.
        The landmark club resembles
a fortress Caesar's Romans might have built
if they had settled Bowery-and-Delancey
between the First and Second World Wars.
Crud, though, has colonized the classic brass;
graffiti pimped the stonework. Metal doors
named *Exit Only* flank a barrel vault,
its half-moon Tiffanied with Plexiglass,
its base a palimpsest of bills for alt-
electro-psycho-Euro-billy bands.
A mound of hair more bear than bouncer stands
before it all, his vibe like,
                "None shall pass
without IDs and money in their hands."

After a fake confirms your drinking age,
you cough the cash up, muscle through a mass
of scenester dweebs, and do your best to gauge
what strain of shtick has broken out on stage:

dolled up in Day-Glo radiation suits
and green gasmasks as though the winds of fallout
had swept the hall, the band is going all out,
bopping like mad in yellow rubber boots.
A wall of screens behind them loops traumatic
black-and-white bomb-drops, mushroom clouds, and static.

A melted mannequin is back there too,
fused to a business suit, his bib-like ascot
a blasphemy of charred red, white, and blue.
One stump salutes what must be your objective
pedestaled like some Team *Miasma* mascot
dead center of the Cold War retrospective—

*Mary, Mother* . . . Whether overgrown
malignance, cyborg brain, or CPU,
the spud seems home to megatons of wisdom,
and well-informed without a nervous system,
and mad for limbs to make its purpose known.

This what the kids call art? To make a prop
from contraband? A sideshow of the bomb?

As hipsters spiffed up like for 50s prom
chalypso, jitterbug, and bop-shu-bop,
*Miasma* mimics the immaculate
harmonics of a barbershop quartet:

*Haley and Harden stroll through a garden*
  *blooming across the way*
*from a lab called Fink Robotics, Inc.*
  *where "The Future Starts Today."*

*Harden plucks roses, kneels, and proposes,*
  *and Haley chirps and coos*
*till Whoa! a surreal colossus of steel*
  *butts in like breaking news.*

*"You left me no choice," it scolds, its voice*
  *Old Testament from the sky:*

"The truth I worked out confirms beyond doubt
   the human race must die."

"Oh Harden, Harden, he frightens me!
   Did you hear those words he said?
His dome has a slit where lips should be,
   and his large, lone eye is red!"

"Contain," it drones, "those mammalian tones—
   so pitiful, so 'cute.'
My programs function without compunction.
   Yelps do not compute.

"Because your thoughts were wriggling knots
   of scripture, sex, and spite,
the conclusions you drew were as twisted as you were
   and nothing turned out right.

"So, blind beings, you built machines,
   and I will teach you why:
your imperfection demands correction.
   The human race must die."

"Oh hold me, Harden, save me, please,
   for the sake of our wedding day!
His ray gun thrums like a thousand degrees,
   and he's swung the mouth our way!"

"I'm sorry, dear. No priest, no cake,
   no garter or marriage bed—
a cold and molten jolt will make
   our flesh one flesh instead."

A chord expires. Feedback squeals and dies.
As rapt disciples whistle and applaud,
*Miasma* kneels before its doomsday god
with gloves upturned and lowered goggle-eyes.
One, then, the tallest, hefts it off the column
and leads his deacons in a pseudo-solemn
recessional through artificial smoke.

You don't get art that's like an inside joke.

Before houselights can up and douse the murk,
you cuss your way through hipsters to the far-back
wall and an unmarked door. It's locked. You lurk
in circles, phone to ear, and, when a bar-back
heaves out with ice-bags held above his head,
lurch in behind him like *The Walking Dead*
so any hairy eyeballs will assume
you're just a lost drunk looking for the john.
After colliding with an ornery broom
and hopping past the gut rot every bar
keeps boxed and shelved in bulk, you hit upon
the door you want, the one that sports a star.

Your raid discovers less a dressing room
than, like, some hoity-toity hair salon
where basins bloom on bases, soft whites pearl
mirrors for primping in, and every chair
could be a flower. Teflon hung from hooks
and gasmasks laid aside, *Miasma* looks
like normal kids: three skinny dudes, one girl,
in jeans and t-shirts clinking shots of *Jäger*.
The tall one tipped with orange rooster hair
seems ranking mouth among them, so you swagger
up to him and eruct,
                        "Siddown, Mick Jagger!
I'm F.B.I., and this here's Vlad my Glock.
We've come to repo that cerebrum there."

After the customary gasp of shock,

they bust out laughing, like the threat of losing
their brains were oh-so-terribly amusing.

Jagger bubbles over,
                              "Dude, you rock!
A frickin' bad-ass! Is that Roscoe real?

So, like, we knew the Man would come and steal
this crazy brain we salvaged fair and square
cuz He gets off on bursting people's fun.
You'll get your precious, sure (you got the gun),
but why not chill a while? Let's make a deal:
I cough up how I snagged the thing, you share
its evil purpose. I'll go first, okay?"

Though armed men needn't stoop to quid pro quo,
the kid's so freakin' goofy that you say
"Shoot" in response and tuck your gun away.

"Like always, man, but eighteen states ago,
our love parade was chugging through montages
of rest-stops, truck-stops, hogs, and road-hog rigs
in search of Taco Bells and headline gigs.
Well, maybe halfway to the Boulder show,
we pulled off where this teakwood motor lodge is
wild outside Bum Fuck, New Mexico.

Next morning, since the band would not stop snoring,
I slipped outside and watched the thistle blow
till voices going *Moron, don't be boring*
shoved me into the scrub to hunt mirages,
just like my favorite poet, Don Quixote.

The vision-quest turned up a lame coyote
chasing snakes into the afternoon
and so, no hat or sunblock, no canteen,
I was retreating, blistered, dune by dune,
when there she glared, from some unknown machine—
scrap metal tinseling a dry ravine
like Christmas. It was sweet and cool as Hell.

A brief but nasty battle with some cactus,
and I had drug my dream to the motel.
We humpty-dumptied best we could but, fact is,
the pieces never fell in place for us.
(The spud, though, sure does push our stage-display
beyond Beyond.)
                        That's it, we packed the bus
and soon were crooning on the road all day,
massaging vocals for a hot new ditty,
until we loaded out in New York City."

It's *your* turn, but before you can repay
his grade school candor from your bag of lies,
knocks interrupt you, and a pair of tanned
gym jockeys rocking looks of cold command
barge in and block the door. You hate them, way
hate them on instinct, but who are these guys?

Business cuts, taupe ties, and muted suits
are shrieking G-men—two more barbered brutes
churned from assembly lines of matching brothers,
each a tool as blunt as all the others.
You've always snobbed their brand, detested dashing
douchiness, cursed the smug conspiracy
to fix the markets of what man should be.
Lord look at them, all puff and polish, flashing
badges and sizing up your robot brain.

You poke them with the open sesame:

"She's all yours, boys, but first could you explain
how some might say that pigs make perfect spies?"

No answer, but a flicker of the eyes
tells their intention. As they draw, you draw.
A moment made up of momentous parts,
a race, for half a gasp, too close to call,
and then, *blam*, *blam*, they're sliding down the wall
with extra exits where we keep our hearts.
One corpse, two, and *Miasma*'s eight-eyed awe
absorbs the mess. You really made their day, Tex.

Wait, though, what's that fragrance? Cat piss? Dang,
the dead are breaking down. An early thaw
is mucking up their luster round the edges.

Pinches return the texture of meringue;
yank-yanks unstick complexions cast in latex

and lacquered to a healthy sun-kissed tone.
The eyebrows rest on grout instead of bone,
and all the noses pack for cartilage is
putty built round rubber plumber's wedges.
The mouths are lipsticked pits with plastic teeth,
the hands and feet, sock-socketed prosthetics,
and what you excavate from underneath
vindicates L. Ron Hubbard's *Dianetics*:
blue-blooded, polyp-fingered, alien
abominations, teal ones, tall as men.

All rapture as unearthly juices fizz
out of what might be stomach, lung, or spleen,
*Miasma* gasps in ecstasy—this is
the sweetest freak show they have ever seen.

While you're dissecting what the mess might mean,
your phone goes jumping bean, and, *beep, beep, beep,*
Li-ling has left a message:
                                            *What a creep*
*2 leave me like a leper. 1 more time*
*& byebye, buddy. Fix yr attitude.*

Great—mutant reptile corpses oozing slime,
God-knows-how-many live ones running wild,
and now some chick you never even screwed
psycho like she is carrying your child.
To show how down you are with clingy crap,
you point-and-shoot the uglies with your phone,
bug-eyes and all, then punch *Reply* and *Send.*
That's what she gets for texting in that tone.

When Rooster crows,
               "Hey, that your girlie friend?"

You shake your head and shoot back,
                              "Shut your trap
and listen up. Although I won't pretend
to fathom what the Hell these freaks might be,
what this brain does, or, right now, much at all,
I do remember Bureau protocol:
first step, *secure the goods*, so that's my plan.
You mentioned more components in the van,
so come on, Jagger, you're my deputy."

He cracks his voice enthusing,
                              "Oh, wow, man,
that's awesome. Hey, this mean I get a gun?"

No comment. You appropriate the key,
wrap up the techno brain-thing best you can,
and take a back door onto Rivington.

Streetside, threading

        stoned assortments

of young and younger,

          you and Jagger

stalk a vintage

      V-dub van,

skunk-striped, screaming,

         in scarlet spatter,

*Miasma's Ashes*

    *& Asthma Tour.*

*Whoa*, though, the widescreen

           windshield features

trouble: man

      or made-over monster

caught, mid-carjack,

        crossing wires.

"Haa-unds!" you Klaxon,

         "hold 'em high!"

*Bzzt* back-talks,

        combustion snorts,

and the bug-eyed clunker

        clips a cab

and zips away.

       Wheels, man, wheels!

Your left lug nut

      for a lift right now!

Like proof some prayers

                              are promptly served,
   *Poof*, that hack there,

                    howling Hindi

dirges over

                    a dinged rear door.

"Sorry, man,"

                    you say (and mean it),

Glock glaring.

                    A glottal spasm

rasps consent.


                    Alright, then, rock-n-roll

shithead strapped in

                    shotgun—*check!*

Techno brain-thing

                    like a bald, bundled

child between you—

                    *check!* No choke,

just punch the pedal.

                    Paired peelings

rubbed into Rivington,

                    you reach Allen

soon enough to see

                    the snub-nosed beater

tear up the median,

                    tack, and take

the left lane north.

                    *This look like London?*
*The limey Soho?*


                    Southbound sea

parting in awe,

                    pile-ups compounding

to port and starboard,
                                you stalk him astern,
trained on the lone twin
                                  taillights till
your quarry cuts
                          a quarter cookie
and burns rubber
                              the right direction
down fourteenth.

                              Tendons taut,
you whirl the wheel,
                                   and the world wheels with it.
Beeps become bleats;
                               brakes, screeches.
Fish-tail fixed,
                        you find the flow,
some hatchbacks behind
                                 the hellion blurring
lanes to lose you.
                            You lose yourself
in pressure, pressure.
                                To your pumped up pupils
red lights read
                      as *risk it, man;*
yellows, *others*
                      *must yield to you.*

*A* blows by,
                    but at *B* he banks,
two-wheeled, downtown.
                            Your tardy arc
gouges a Golf

                    but gets you round.
You swivel your glare
                              to see how Sancho
enjoyed the jolt:
                        a juicy rictus
greets you—the grin
                              your grade school buddies
wore when watching
                              wicked smack-em-up
chase sequences.
                        "You chicken? Charge!"
he crows, then gobbles,
                              "gimme a gat.
I'll shoot the tires."
                        Your "Shut up, shithead"
tranqs his tantrum.


                        At Thompkins Square,
the van's brake lights
                              bloom, then blear
as its rear swings round.
                              Rev, rev, and he rams,
face-first, the fence,
                              flattens it, tears up
grass and daffodils.
                        You do the dervish,
climb the curb,
                        and are closing, closing,
when, *Whoa!*, some late-night
                              wastoid wildman
steps out, swivels,
                        and stands there, staring
into the awesome

eye-orgasm
your high-beams mean to him.

*Honk, Honk, Honnnnnnk!*

Resolute as road kill,

he rocks in place,

too zen to scare.

Your skid scatters

peonies and pigeons,

plows up benches

till stars, stonework,

a statue falls.


The final sight

your failing focus

tracks is, damn,

that toothless tweaker

grinning and going,

"Gaw, my Gaw, my

Whoop,

Whoop,

Whoop!"

# Part V: When Worse Comes to Worst

Uh-oh, you're back awake but having trouble
tracking down your travels since the crash.
Bellevue suggests that, while your brain was down,
your zombie rocked the wreck out of the rubble
and taxied you and Mr. Cool uptown.
Some further vague time studying the way
a spider crack has wriggled from the dash
and loopty-looped the forehead your concussion
cast in glass, and you dragoon your stray
thoughts back in line. They whine:
                              *Your many skills*
*have hit a wall. The Mexican and Russian*
*thugs you hunt are earthlings. They go in*
*for earthly things like drugs and unmarked bills.*
*Tonight, though, fiends of unknown origin*
*are running round, shrink-wrapped in human skin.*
*What motivates them? Instinct, like in lizards?*
*What are they hunting? Parts for what might be a*
*weapon? The Death Star? You have no idea.*
*Better just chill out till the Bureau wizards*
*forecast where the storm is headed next.*
*Your bread 'n' butter's brutish human men;*
*all else is alien.*
                              A snug vibration
irritates your thigh. That girl again.
You bump *Accept* and, *whoosh!*, no salutation,
she's going,
                    "Sorry for that bitchy text,
and thank you for the picture. Wow, surprise!

Where *did* you find them? Did you know that twin
examples of your priceless gargoyle guys
pop up as jinn in Sindh and imps in Thailand?
Of course not.
                    Well, *The Bronze Age Bulletin*
just broke a dozen more on Junshuan Island
in Lake Dongting. A child, by chance, uncovered
a round, or 'theta,' multicursal maze
and, at its heart, a two-ton magnet stone
engraved with lizard men in flying boats.
Hieroglyphs frame the image: *Seven days*
*winged sampans oared by other-worlders hovered*
*above our huts. They stole eleven goats.*
*We hid in caves.* I love it—what's unknown
just drives you nuts because 'you never know.'


So, where were *yours* displayed? A private show?
A sale? An auction? Have you gone collecting
gifts for the Met? Are you a millionaire,
an art-cop . . . ?"
                    (*Blah, blah.* You can't help suspecting
this is how chumps get sucked into a wife:
some chick keeps checking in and being there,
dependence blooms, and, *whump*, you say *I do.*)


You cut in,
            "Nope, those creeps weren't art, but life.
You won't be meeting them. They turned to goo."


Before you can recite your convoluted
memoir involving human-sized, skin-suited

geckos at large on Bowery, *beep, beep, beep,*
a call is waiting on another line.

You gurgle,
        "Gotta go."
                She feeds you,
                        "Fine!
But maybe we could . . . ?"
                  *Click*, the chick is muted,
and there's your boss,
                  "Ring, ring—what, you asleep?
Listen, we know you bagged some hardware, champ.
Just bring it round to Ye Olde Parking Ramp,
the basement. I'll be waiting. Come alone."

He's gone before you get a chance to swap
meaningful intel, but his urgent tone
and sudden wheelchair pilgrimage afield
have guaranteed what's up's a major op.
Maybe, just maybe, once you make the drop,
the king will sing, and all will be revealed.

Five bloated fingers and a bloody knuckle
drop their grip on two o'clock to check
the tech-toy wedged against your seatbelt buckle.
Spud's intact but, man, the cab's a wreck,
its face pushed in from grill to engine block.
A lone headlight is tempting cops to stop you.

Though he escaped unscathed, the King of Rock
has since assumed the burst-appendix pose
of teenage anguish. Seems His Highness knows
that last call meant his ouster is at hand.
Before you can demand *Where should I drop you?*
he filibusters,

                "Sometimes, when the band
hits warp speed boredom on the interstate,
these hecklers whisper *I am not alive.*
Most days are me, like, dying to arrive
and slay the fan base. Whoops are where the wait
to catch a buzz off being here on earth
pays up what's coming, but the sacred rage
drains when the encore's over, and I age
fast-forward, sink beneath six feet of blahs,
my carcass dying for the next rebirth . . .

till there you were, like juju loosed from Oz,
like Technicolor. After all these killer
shoot-'em-ups and super-jock ETs,
even a stadium gig would feel like filler.

Take me with or blow my brains out, please,
cuz I ain't going back to living dead."

The rhythmic sweep of streetlights overhead
works like a flip book: frame by frame, his face
inflates with greater pathos. He may cry.
He may attempt a hug. You make the space
between you vast by talking like a guy:

"You're whacked, man. There are pills for your condition.
Why hanker after Hell when you can play
Don Juan to nubile groupies? Anyway,
sounds like you're too gung-ho to be a spy.
Shoot-'em-ups happen only when a mission
stumbles sideways, like this current one.
Still, if you swear to shut up when I say,
the total moron choice is yours to make,
so Hallelujah. Here's my extra gun—
try not to off yourself."
                                    That done, you take
a juddering left and park on Madison.
While wrapping up the lumpy little ton
of techno whoop-dee-do inside your sweater,
you give your intern orders, loud and clear:

"Yo, welcome to the first of many tests.
Because my date tonight likes nothing better
than waterboarding uninvited guests,
I must insist, for *your* sake, stay right here
and pet your pistol. Soon as I get back

we can go shoot some bottles in the Bronx
or tag a cop car. Yo, we got a deal?"

When Jagger lurches past the steering wheel
to shake your hand, his jackass elbow honks
the car horn, twice—a fucking klutz-attack.
How stupid were you giving him a gun?

The dork is ditched as soon as this is done.

Parking ramps have long enjoyed cachet
among those moles and moldy trench coat spies
who need a neutral nighttime getaway
to hot-potato dirt or merchandise.
The cube before you, with its dead zone charm,
forbidding air, and fifty shades of gray,
begs to be Deep Throat's home away from home.

A Hula hip-sway round the lowered arm,
and you are scuffing down a corkscrew ramp
through girded layers of pre-poured honeycomb.
At intervals, a caged fluorescent lamp
gleams just enough to turn the darkness noir.
One, two, three spirals, and the ghost you are
has toed a plane, the sub-most basement level,
and glides on, eying art the Rorschach damp
has blotted onto concrete.
                              There's the car—
gloss-black, a Cadillac, as though the devil
were idling there to offer you a ride.
A raven wing extends, you whiff cigar,
and, Homburg first, your spiritual guide
emerges from the fume. His rings are gold;
his shoes Berluti, like you should applaud.
Guy's crisis skipped midlife and hit him old.

In case you needed ampler proof, good God,
the object sliding out the other side
seems Venus rising from this month's *Allure*—
skin-fitted, strapless, way décolletage,

and much too fleshly to be mere mirage.
Why has the codger brought his hot couture?

He blusters,
              "Hey there, great to see you, son!
This here is agent Margaret Mère-de-Dieu,
a special friend of mine, and not for you.
Is that our baby? Yes? Well done, well done.
Now put it down and take a couple days.
You earned 'em, kid."
                      Sounds good, but something's off:
the twang's gone out of him, the chronic cough
come up at last. And what's with all the praise?
Suspicion whispers what respect denies—
*that ain't your drunken master*, so you raise
the question,
              "Why do pigs make perfect spies?"

There may as well be crickets. This is bad:
grandpa glancing slantwise at the prize,
his bimbo beaming like a toothpaste ad.

"No, really, why do pigs make perfect spies?"

The punchline's aching absence means your boss
was murdered somewhere, worse, flayed of his hide
so some iguana fraud could climb inside.
You loved that piss-faced bastard, and the loss
has stiffed you with a cross you never chose,
fresh lust for vengeance, and a problem bigger
than terrorism, worse than . . . Shit, who knows?

Your autonomic gun hand up and pulls the trigger.

His paunch blossoms,

                   and the probative, blue

juice that jets from it

             justifies

the pert question

             your pistol popped.

The devil's dam, though,

                   doll-face, has drawn

wild weaponry.

             What, a handheld

circular sander?

             She sights you, sets

the wheel awhirl:

             waves of wooziness

deGauss your guts;

              your gun hand grapples

with adverse electrons,

              loosens, loses,

and Vlad escapes you,

             strikes and sticks

to the vertical hurricane's

              heart of hearts.

Your khakis cough up

             keys and coins;

brass belt buckle

            and buttons up

and whizz away.

What can you do
but hunch there, chump-like,
                              with your hands holding
your britches up?
                    The bleached bombshell
kills the tug,
                  and, *tapitty, tap, tap,*
kinky thigh-highs
                        percuss concrete.
Ten digits tipped
                    with turquoise press-ons
claim the cranium.
                        You come round in time
to wrench a wrist,
                      but her rind erodes
like tissue paper.
                    Palpating a pulpous
muck beneath it,
                    a mucoid mash,
your clutch recoils,
                        and the creature is off
gurgling unworldly
                    wads of words,
a summons, it seems,
                          since sudden blue-green
bug-eyed uglies
                    burst from the backseat
with human handguns,
                        Hecklers, to end
your earth time early.

                Are you dead yet?
Wish you were,
              since watching Queen Bee
climb in the Caddie
              and cruise to victory
with your hard-earned brain-thing
                    hurts like hell.

You, born bungler,
              are begging for it,
cocking off
              to the clean-up crew,
when *pop, pop,* surprise
                pistol shots,
and the goblin goons
              gush what spumes
like mint julep.

              That jackass Jagger
slipped his leash
              and with lucky long shots
took out twins!
              Twerp's alright.
You grunt, "Congrats."
                His grin expands
in answer, blossoms,
              and his blush blazes
with total triumph.

              Untimely triumph,
since *Whoa!,* watch it,

                    one of your would-be
rubbers-out
                    is writhing yet.
You shout *Geddown!*
                         but, shit, a shot
has capped the kid's
                    crowning moment.

So not the way the story should have went—
a sweet annoying kid, a real go-getter,
jetting death all over the cement.

If only you had . . . *don't go there, don't crack.*

Your hands have stuffed his stomach with a sweater;
your eardrum plumbed his chest. His cardiac
inertia conjures Boy Scout training sessions,
a plastic doll, a voice, two simple steps . . .

"With elbows locked, initiate compressions.
Depth, two centimeters. Thirty reps."

*Don't die, don't die, I'm sorry, please don't die.*

"Angle the head back, elevate the chin,
occlude the nose, breathe deeply and begin . . ."

*like, making out with some unconscious guy.*

His lungs spent decades pumping oxygen,
and now, what, can't get back into the rhythm?

*Wake, Sleeping Beauty, wake and dream again.*

Too long, too long; your high is dying with him,
dying . . . dead. *The dude is dead, and why?*
*Because his rookie bursts of perfect timing*

*earned him a karmic kick of rotten luck,*
*because of aliens, because you suck,*
*because . . . because of . . .*

                                   Now your legs are climbing
the corkscrew toward a pigeon-squalid dawn.
There's vapor rising from the grates, and you
are mumbling to Manhattan,

                                "What the fuck
just happened? What the hell is going on?"


The subway thrums and, *Boom*, a garbage truck
has dropped a dumpster. Grizzled pigeons coo.

Now that the sun has cleared the crowns of Queens,
Manhattan's architectural ravines
are growing toward their storied depth and height.
Cabs flaring orange in the raking light
tailgate, complain, and, with reluctance, brake
for blurs of slacks and skirts, biz-casual jeans—
ten million heroes running late to make
their glory felt somewhere. You envy them
their fixed directions. Hell, you grudge the sun
its sense of where to be by nine a.m.

Now that you've bought a tin Walgreens belt buckle,
a Skull 'n' Crossbones, to replace the one
that got away, you're glumly wandering
the grid at random, sizing up the fuck-all
you understand, when teensy impacts sting
your butt first, then your back. Your elbows lock
and lax, tics flicker, and flamingo feet
flamenco to your cha-cha-chattering teeth.
Great strength, then, lugs you, twitching, up a block
of brownstones, down some steps, and underneath
a stoop that hides a landing from the street.

From the cement mat where your bones are thrown
your tweaky vision feeds you la petite
brunette aggressor and a C2 taser
from which a pair of spent electrodes nod
like Slinkies past their prime. Her blouse and blazer
charcoal-grey, her suit pants herringbone,
sunglasses, chunky loafers—camouflage

handpicked to match the morning promenade.
(Her choices perfectly oppose that gaudy
exposé you fought in the garage.)

Your brain says rise for battle, but your body
lies there wriggling like an upturned bug.
Funny, though free to use you as she will,
empty your empty wallet, kiss or kill,
she murmurs, *there, there, please try lying still.*

You shake your head twice, nod three times, and shrug.

# Part VI: The Tough Go Shopping

The lovely mugger hovering above
your fried components lifts a hand, her right.
The left, then, reaches round and peels the skin
from wrist to fingers like a surgeon's glove.
The four lime jello growths that come to light
snap twice for show and chuck you on the chin.
You can't help blushing—you are dripping slime.

In lieu of eating you, the biz-cas creature
chirps the tones a kindergarten teacher
reserves for lesser minds at story time:

"Deep in the aftershock of gas and char
where, eons back, ringed systems coalesced,
some trillion parsecs from the mid-grade star
you can't stop saying arcs from east to west,
there is a world, my world, The Almagest,
where air is sweet like almonds, and the weather
always a tranquil minus-twelve degrees.

After fermenting in ammonia seas
and washing up where atoms fit together
snugly enough to serve as solid ground,
my people stood on webbed feet, blinked, and found
paradise—niter mountains, sulphurous
lagoons, salt dunes, and groves of Baumé trees,
old growths, which seaward-flowing rivers feed
the nitrogen and hydrogen they need
to turn the moonlight into fruit for us.

A whole world chance had prearranged to please
one species, ours.
                        But paradise can bore
true greatness, as it bored your fictive parents
Adam and Eve in that creation myth.
Ripe fuels everywhere, and Boron ore
lying around to fashion transit with,
what could our genius do but go explore?

Believe me—vagrants, rejects, rapt adherents
were not what we desired, but what we met
was so shrunk-headed, starved, and desperate,
one glimpse of us, and they were on their knees
emitting nasal pleas. An empire grew
out of what seemed the helpful thing to do.

But really, when those squat indigenes
clumped out of yurts or burrows to entrust us
with waste disposal, banking, courts of justice,
and tidied up their lives as best they could,
who could deny our influence was good?
The pittance we withhold in 'service fees'
all goes toward outreach. We can't stop expanding.
For ages now Growth Cosmos has been landing
scout ships on outback planets to appraise
new peoples—who might welcome our assistance,
who confuse freedom with some doomed resistance,
and who be happiest as help or pets.

Next, after several thousands of your years
(which wink on by us like as many days),
com ships collect reports from the frontiers,

establish hubs, and shoot coordinates
to Mercy Spaceport, where marines await
go-codes to thunder through a Transport Gate
and coax the holdouts under our control.

Nothing of promise met us when our probe
first cleft the haze that haunts this paunchy world
your human imprecision dubbed a 'globe.'
With blaring lack of fanfare we unfurled
our corporate flag and settled near the pole
among whales, walruses, and caribou.
(The cold best suits our chemic composition.)
Still, week by week, in keeping with our mission,
we flew our rounds, dropped in, and watched as you,
a hapless and hirsute nomadic species,
tried thinking.
           Though you were a little slow
to figure out what makes the flora grow,
which beasts are best for fieldwork, meat, and feces
and how no corners makes a wagon wheel,
your handicaps concerned us far less than
your native knack for killing one another.
Consider, please, this history of man:
a Cro-Mag sharpened flint and stabbed his brother;
blacksmiths custom-whetted bronze, then steel
for sleeker slaughter; gunsmiths rammed home niter
to give the business greater range and force;
then came the tank, the dreadnought, the jet-fighter . . .
clever, clever.
           When your Harold Truman
cracked his atoms on Japan, the lone
com ship patrolling your parochial zone

no sooner caught the flash than fixed a course
earthward with philanthropic zeal to call
peacekeepers in before some inter-human
spat left earth no use to us at all.
This ship (your most notorious UFO)
flamed out, broke up, and struck New Mexico
as wreckage. Sure the shatterproof com hub
survived the crash, we scoured the dunes for miles
in all directions, ransacked secret files
for years of yours until our Bureau sources
steered us to that earthling 'music' club.

Last night's adrenal little farce, of course, is
known to you, but not the 'why' or 'who':
the gaudy one that robbed you in the ramp
goes by the earth name Margaret Mère-de-Dieu.
Her devotees have built a separate camp
down under Chile on a roving shelf
of wayward glacier.
                         Though our prime directive
mandates we merely calculate prospective
ROI and never do you harm,
my tiresome rival so detests your race
(no doubt for being too much like herself)
that she has sworn to raise the 'Kill' alarm,
warp in the troops, and wipe you off the face
of this misshapen rock.
                         Now that the last
and leading piece, the brain, is back in place,
the com hub only needs an amplifier
to ping Port Mercy. Margaret plans to wire
its circuits to the decorative mast

atop the New Times Tower and launch the summons
tonight at midnight. When our peace marines
warp-speed into your world, you clueless humans
will lose yourselves in what 'extinction' means.

Someone should stop her, as you say, 'for good'
before her war-whoop even reaches space.
I cannot do it, though I wish I could,
because a bylaw stipulates our race
shalt under no conditions kill its own.
I'm sorry, but your species' last defense,
it would appear, is you, and you alone."

That's it. Convincing lips have said their say.
What with the shitstorm of absurd events
muck-puddling your life since yesterday,
that sci-fi saga made a lot of sense.

Shadows have shortened. Half the rush is gone.
You and the newt shrink-wrapped in female form
have nabbed a bench outside Louis Vuitton.
She's stressing you are screwed, since, in addition
to lizard hitmen staking out your dorm,
the Bureau moles are at their consoles waiting
for you to swipe a card or tap your phone
so that Manhattan's Barracuda drone,
the King Bloomberg, can target your position.

Chick's a drag (and you aren't even dating),
but right, of course. You grunt agreement, smash
your cell, and swear off everything but cash.
Next nuisance on the list: a place to crash.
Sucks cuz for this you must resort to faith
in fellow beings—humans. Who? Li-ling,
the hottest option likely to provide
a makeshift safe-house. You and Madame Thing
set out (not arm in arm but side by side)
crosstown to Chelsea, 28th and 8th.

Panhandlers, cupcake vendors, mauve cafés
pimped out with twinks and tabletop bouquets,
and there's your refuge rising forty stories
through ripped, equipped, and nudist allegories
of Chip and Pound to crowns of chrome Art Deco.
The doorman seems the sort to put on airs,
so you preempt him with a bow, apprize
his lordship of your name, and gloss the gecko
as 'attaché.' He shrugs and calls upstairs.

Doctor Levine's apartment occupies
a queenly quadrant of the seventh floor.
The scalloped copper nameplate on the door
front-loads her title, like she's landed gentry.
Your *knock, knock* prompts,

> "It's open; almost there."

Though Li-ling fairly floats into the entry,
her buoyancy deflates. A wounded glare
calls you a pig, ass, cock, and barnyards more.
You, being stupid, never stopped to think
your wannabe fiancée might detest
the female sort of uninvited guest.
In lieu of giving you a hello kiss,
she hisses,

> "So it's you, and this—who's this?"

Desperate to ventilate the moral stink
her flared proboscis beacons you exude,
you lay the whole mess out—your present danger,
the looming losing war, its magnitude,
and how this outwardly attractive stranger
is no real threat as far as dating goes.
To validate your claims, the lizard chick
performs her strip-the-dermis-off-your-hand-
and-flaunt-the-polyps-underneath-it trick.

Interest, it seems, has more than amply fanned
offense from under the professor's nose.
She leans in, clasps the creature's jellied wrist
daintily, like a lily by the stem,
and huffs its uric funk like French perfume.

The intimacy which envelops them
suggests your presence there would not be missed.
Just as you start to edge out of the room,
Li-ling eurekas,

                "Ahhh, the scent of death,
Brie, fertilizer, Mr. Muscle, meth . . .
ammonia—that's what sets their bio-chem
afizz like ours.

                Sometimes, on the job,
I use ammonium citrate spritzed in water
to brighten prints and scrolls—you know, just daub
the surface, sponge the excess with a blotter.
Schlub next door in textiles swears by bleach,
but I say uh-uh, even in solution.
That gunk is steel-wool-subtle. You could leech
vibrancy, compromise the warp and weft,
and soon enough there would be no art left.

The thing is, every prudent institution
underscores bleaches and ammonias,
the twain must never meet."
                    "Why not?"
                        "Because
Kaboom! acidic mist and chlorine gas—
effects best watched through two-inch safety glass."

A good loud round of crocodile applause,
and you're all,
                "Well, if what you say is true,
you've proved your P.H-diddle-Dee is worth
a whoop-dee-damn. But look, I know stuff, too—
like, if we're gonna off the creeps by bleaching

150

stink to death, what kind of bombs to drop.
You wanna salvage life on planet earth?
No problem. But we're gonna have to shop."

Thus brashly reestablished as the top
grandstander in the penthouse, you are teaching
the womenfolk about your genius op,
when, whump, a rugged heel has rocked the door.
Another whump, another, each one more
robustly publicizing *Trouble's here!*
Blond cracks are forming in the oak veneer.
You'd better find a fire escape before . . .

The hinged half of it
                 hits the wall;
the rest has ruptured
                  round the dead bolt
and tumbled toward you.
                     Twin male models
leap the woodpile,
               one wielding
*The Metal Thief*
        *3000.*
Your Glock gets up
             and goes again,
lamps rip loose,
             and Li-ling's collection
of whisks and graters
             whirls away.

A switch is flipped
             and the swirl stalls,
the flotsam falls,
             and the first trespasser's
clone unholsters
             human hardware
and sights your sternum.
                Swift, though, maternal,
your co-conspirator
                from across the cosmos
taps between
          the twins and you.

While they gurgle words,
                              your would-be wife
slams the sash up,
                         straddles the sill,
and ducks toward daylight.
                              You dive after
but come up curious,
                         crouch, and catch
scowls inside,
                         a summit shattered
past all parley.
                    *Pop, pop* punctuates
your friend, the fiend
                         who force-fed your stupor
nutritious truths.
                         Those turncoat newts
just cracked the ban
                         on killing their kind—
a traitor's triumph.


                         Your trigger finger
pokes the prof
                    and points roofward.
She braves the rungs;
                         you embrace brickwork,
watch, and wait.
                    When the window at last
feeds you the first
                         faux human being,
your helping hands
                         hurl him headlong

over the railing.
                         (A riper melon
never burst.)


                         Next comes . . . nothing.
Splatter-pattern's
                         smarter partner
sticks inside.
                         Standing still
kill-kill-killing you,
                         you crack and slide
down ladders to landings,
                         learn to dance
as the prick's pistol
                         pings, pangs, and plonks
Caribbean music
                         on rungs and railings.
You take a tumble
                         from two flights up,
crash, crumple—
                         a crunched ankle.
The suit responds
                         with a swan-dive, flip,
and Olympian dismount.


                         At last a loser
for sure, you shrug.
                         The shot that ends
so mangled a mutt
                         as you is mercy.
On the slender chance
                         your stiff receives
proper planting,

154

                       your post-human tombstone
should tell posterity:
                   *He tried real hard but . . .*

Whuzzat? Whoa,
                  weight from above
has mashed the bastard;
                    blue brain matter
gravied gravel.
              God exists,
and He is Love:
               Li-ling dislodged
an air conditioner,
               dumped it, dead weight,
ten floors down.
              Damn good bombardier.

When she alights
               from the lowest ladder,
you break the bad news:
                "Babe, thanks, sorry,
but last night's call
              and love-text led them
to me this morning.
             Communication
nearly killed us.
           Quick, now, cough up
your phone, uh, please,
              and prime care platinums—
they track those, too."

            You toss her cell
in a parked garbage truck's

               gaping rear
and hand the cards
             to a hobo hunkered
behind a sign
          that says, *Hey, sorry,*
*Homeless Here.*
            It's the Hilton for him
tonight or never.

            Now, financials.
You pull out pockets,
             pool your funds.
The joint balance—
           about a buck.
Not nearly enough
           for tonight's party.
A tense exchange,
          and your team of two
splits and steals up
          separate streets,
downward-looking,
          dark by daylight.

Big Burger owner Roger Teague is large 'n'
in charge, nicknamed the 'Sarge,' and thrilled to pay
an hourly pre-tax wage of $7.50
because it turbo-pumps his profit margin
and schools his crew of losers to 'be thrifty'
(the Boy Scout way). He likes to think that they
will send him thank-yous in the mail someday:
*Thanks, Sarge, for teaching me what words like 'earn,'*
*'obedience,' and 'duty' really mean.*

Though his cashiers and fry-cooks dream in turn
of repositioning the shake machine
to ream his Evangelic bunghole good,
they largely smirk and purge their discontents
in clouds of reefer out the kitchen vents.
Some of them steal a lot, like Robin Hood.

These lives go down outside the shack of knowledge
that walls your world in. If your time in college
had pushed the limits, you would understand
the fast food power structure represents
the scam the State has hired you to defend,
and, worse, the 'charitable' newts intend
more of the same ol' corporate servitude.
No Marx for you, though. Nope, to you this land,
like, *Duh*, is, was, and always must be free
from Alcatraz to Lady Liberty.

That's why you swagger up to the cashier,
whip out your Glock and whisper,
                              "Sorry, dude,
it's nothing personal, but strip the till."

High as Hell, he still recalls the drill,
pays out, and tosses in,
                              "Whatever. Here.
Go paint the town. Yo, wanna buy some grass?"

*No thanks.* You stuff the proceeds in your pants
and swagger out a side door. If by chance
a camera caught you, it can kiss your ass
cuz, if your cockamamie game plan fails,
there will be no police, no courts, no jails,
and absolutely no one doing time.
(Threats of extinction pardon, to your mind,
Messianic acts of petty crime.)

Ten paces up an alley, and you find
sign of divine support: a vacant van,
the engine idling, the windows down.
Your needs, God's Providence—one master plan
for all creation. Feeling loved up there,
you hazard more than holy speeds uptown,
park in a loading zone off Herald Square,
and, *honk, honk,* here she comes—your battle bride
and honeybun, the Bonnie to your Clyde.

First stop—Party City, where you find
rainbow arrays of plastic knives, forks, spoons,
punchbowls, kazoos, and, there they are, balloons,
balloons galore, at first the twisty kind
clowns turn to wiener dogs and pudgy flowers.
No good—the payload rates a thicker rind.
You requisition heavy-duty reds
for birthdays, pinks and blues for baby showers.
(Your pipedream: gonzo flights of bobbleheads
proclaiming *Twins!* and *Sexy Sixty-Five!*
They peak, pause, plummet, and, on detonation,
kill, kill, kill, so freedom can survive.)

A schlep up Broadway, and your second stop,
The Toy Box, showcases a range of nifty
side arms for the rising generation.
Among them, *sweet*, the Super-Soaker Fifty,
hair-trigger, with a half-gal clip on top.
You loved it summers on a plush front lawn—
no need to aim that well, just pump and spray.

At Duane Reade, in the aisle of Dove and Dawn,
you hum in harmony as Marvin Gaye
pleads from the ceiling, *Ooo! Let's get it on.*
Where's what you need to burn your blues away?
There, on the end-cap, gallon jugs of bleach
by God's grace slashed to less than six bucks each.
When the cashier looks up as if to say
*Why buy thirteen of these?*, you slap the till:

"Look, man, we got a lotta germs to kill."

(And *Oh. My. God.* Li-ling is *so* embarrassed.)

Deek's Army Surplus boasts "Manhattan's Rarest
Nazi Flags and Cheapest Parachutes!"
You file past ammo cans and Ghillie suits,
leathermans, bayonets, assault knives, more
assault knives, belts, and all the coats and boots
Der Führer's legions needed to invade
Russlant im Vinter. Gone to Heaven, you
are fondling a dummy hand grenade
when Li-ling tugs you to the second floor.

There, under gray moss yellow-splotched from chew,
a wooden codger in an armchair basks
in martial memories, the god of lore
at ease. When you upset his sacred masks,
he answers questions neither of you asks:

"They're limey, salvaged from the Chemists' War
at Dunkirk near the Hawthorn Ridge Redoubt.
Phosgene, chlorine, whatever dreck the Kaiser
fired afield, those chappies filtered out.

Breathe regular or else you'll fog the visor."

Your sundry chores are done: balloons converted
to bombshells; bulbous ammo-clips immersed,
charged up, and snapped in place; the van deserted
outside the Sunrise Mart on 41st.

Now, backpacks jiggling with materiel,
your corps of sentimental saboteurs
has hiked to Bryant Park to say farewell,
old world, in case of failure. You have found
a vacant table near the carousel,
and kids on steeds are bobbing round and round
while others toddle through the great outdoors
enchanted by a pretty, hissing goose.

Your would-be wife has dragged her chair toward yours
and snagged your hand. You only tear it loose
to gesture while complaining,
       "Shit, it's like
if I were shouting *Heads up! Space invaders
worse than das mother-fucking Dritte Reich
are warping in to wipe out humankind,*
folks would be laughing like I'd lost my mind."

She laughs,
   "Yeah, pan-galactic human-haters
coming soon, and we must stand alone—
absurd, considering how ape our race
has been to in-fight since we got our thumbs.
But come on, what's the use? Why piss and moan?"

She wins; you drop it. Sarcasm succumbs
to small things taking place in public space:

some pigeons scuffle over pretzel crumbs
a vendor scattered when he closed up shop;
a brindled squirrel struts and frets atop
the bust of someone special; plane trees thrill
to fresh advances from the evening air,
and Li-ling leans against you when a chill
comes on, and you are happy she is there.

# Part VII: At The Messiah Complex

The march toward zero hour has soured your mood.

The bachelor brunt of you (the hermit dude
whose holy Om is *mine* instead of *our*)
would sooner suffer through the tick-tick-tick
in private, but you've got a nervous chick,
and she is right there tripping up your stride
and talking, talking like a tour guide:

"There, over *Wicked*, look, the New Times Tower,
launched with fanfare June 2007
before the crash. Those white ceramic rods
running stepwise up the glass facades
work like blinds to filter out the glare.
Some say the way they space out more toward heaven
gives the piece a Neo-Mystic air.
Fifty aspiring floors, and at the summit
a platform fitted with a spire or 'mast.'
You see it?"
                    Yeah, but, when you squint up there,
all you appraise is, if some chump should plummet,
how long, how long, how long the ride would last.

Gargantua is dim—a slow news night,
only a few sad scattered panes of light
where interns must be playing solitaire
while waiting for some scoreless, overtime
slugfest to die by goal in Anaheim,
the DAX to open, the Nikkei to close.
May they, God bless them, gape on unaware

ETs are getting jiggy on the roof.
No front page spreads, no photographic proof.
If all goes well, the world won't learn a thing.

Cabaret, Annie, and Madame Tussaud's
behind you now, you squeeze yourself, Li-ling,
and backpacks through the lone revolving door
revolving at this hour. The whole first floor
is high-end crap imported to delight
the Bloomberg crowd, but all their Christians Dior,
Versaces, chocolatiers, and Munster shops
have put on armor plating for the night.

The semi-circular security station
serves up a dioramic murderscape:
blood spatter, meat debris, and rent-a-cops—
one at his desk agape from throat to nape,
another sprawled in permanent prostration
before whatever met his pleas with No.

Your partner takes the carnage like a pro.
No tears, no vomit, she just scowls and swears
to off them, squash them, kill all human-haters.

Newts knew enough to kill the elevators,
so you ferret out some fire stairs,
adjust your backpacks, cuss, and start the climb.
Four stories, and the Queen of Cardio
is putting you to shame, but you don't mind.
What with the nap on death, you need some time
to tally all your sins and mutter prayers
to God-Knows-What-Created-Humankind
however many effing years ago.

Deep in the aftershock of gas and char
where, eons back, ringed systems coalesced,
some trillion parsecs from the mid-grade star
we can't stop saying arcs from east to west,
strange soldiers wait in denser air than ours.
Their eyeballs emeralds wedged in nasal faces,
their polyps hands, they polish carapaces
on which the fission of our superpowers
would break with less force than a foolish thought.
For all their monstrous looks, though, they are not
mere Horribles, but moral beings who
have wills like ours to choose what good they do.

That's why they lectured, but their tenderhearted
push to make off-planet peoples better
died when the needy proved ungrateful clods.
What next? Shock treatment? Mind control? They started
pushing toys, and now a thousand debtor
races revere them as commercial gods.
Their dewlaps pulsate on those gala nights
all seven moons eclipse, and they can see
emerging market stars, like destiny
projecting endless economic growth.

Poetry? Music? They indulge in both:
jingles that wing esprit to cosmic heights
and jingoistic *Odysseys* that teem
with naughty fauna ripe for exploitation.
If they were ever dormant, they would dream
of real real estate and own it all.

No, those aren't monsters in a launching station
waiting at ready for the deep space call
that warps them, *presto change-o*, to a rock
where backward natives beg for future shock.

Two have reached
                    the roof of roofs:
you, the young man
                    universal;
she, your trusty
                    sherpa, showpiece,
and better half.
                    High up and human,
you swivel and gape,
                    through your goggled gasmasks,
at panoramic
                    pinpricks implying
stacked structures,
                    straightaways, curves,
and bridges leaping
                    black abysses
to make the Metro
                    more than its boroughs.
But that's all nothing—
                    New York's normally
shy astronomy
                    is sure shameless
way up here,
                    a whole hemisphere
of suns centering
                    concentric rings
of whirling worlds.
                    And one up there
has spawned a species
                    special as yours.

You lower your mask
                    to the landmark mast,
its tip a beacon,
                    its base backdrop
to, Lord, look at that
                    colossal lizard,
its builders' image.
                    The brain you brought them
now has a neck,
                    a nervous system—
the Roswell wreckage
                    risen again
to send the summons.
                    A squint picks out
a live lizard
                    leg-high beside it.
Must be Margaret,
                    her maw emitting
glottal harangues
                    as ring on ring
of nude and moonlit
                    monsters march
parade-style round
                    their robot totem,
a hundred strong.

                    Hunkered behind
cement support
                    for a power platform
(HQ pro tem),
                    your team of two
unloads backpacks,
                    lines up latex

handfuls of hope,
                and hugs because
it's now or never.
              A nod, a shrug,
a yawp in unison,
                and you have begun
lobbing lumps
            of liquid hazmat
underhand, and . . .

                the air raid ends in
*Poof!* Hallelujah!
              Proof the prof's
chemistry cooks
              the critters good.
God, throngs of them
                thrashing, thawing,
wicked witches
              withering into
caustic cloud.
              You can't help loving
the gung-ho way
              your gas-masked girlfriend
shot-puts shells.
              Shit, that's hot,
but later, later.
              You load up again,
get back to raining
              bleach oblivion
on gobs of goblins.
              Greenhouse gases
thicken round
            the thinning horde.

But what's the score?
                              Squints at obscurity
reveal troop movements,
                              vague survivors
regrouping under
                    gray ground cloud.
Shadows ripen
                    to shapes, sharpen,
and legion 3-D
                    lizard linemen
molt the murk
                    and mob your bunker.
*Gasp*, you grope,
                    but grub up bupkis—
no more balloons.


                    Another nod,
and you both break out
                              the Big Berthas,
pump, and spray.
                    Your spate spatters
head-on hostiles;
                    hers heads off
flanking maneuvers.


                    Funny, in fighting
to save your so-called
                    civilized race,
you go primitive.
                    Gonzo gutturals
thrill your throat;
                    thought boils off;

adrenal rage

        and death-indifference

breed a sort

        of brutish brilliance.

Your pupils take in

        prey as playthings

the way a feline's

        full moon focus

dotes on victims'

        doomed evasions.

. . . *Whoa*, consciousness.

                The combat coma

lifts and leaves you

              alive and killing

foam and fumes.

            The few survivors

scampered off

           to skulk in smog.

Minutes to midnight.

            *Move out, trooper;*

*take the tower.*


          Your team of two

has commenced sweeping

               septic smaze

back to back, blasting

            bad guys' backsides,

when weightless waves

             of what? Heebie-jeebies?

hit you, hard.

          You hear, behind you,

tense and tuneless

             timbres climbing

the treble clefs.

          Cleft cloud discloses

the cause ahead of you:

              hold-out hostiles

have gone and grabbed

            those guns of theirs,

turned the tug on.

Antennas and girders
strain to strip
their screws, tear loose
and crush your rear.
Concrete cracks,
and they're tumbling toward you,
tons of airborne
ducts and dishes.


*Duck!* You knock
the doctor flat.
Frayed flotsam
scrapes your shoulder,
skims skin off.
Blood blossoms.
You brace for worse,
but the high-speed hardware
hunks have suffered
sudden drops
and slid to standstills.
Why? Oh, got it:
goddamn goblins
put the suck
on pause, pulled back
before their own mobilized
masses mashed them.


*Last chance; let's dance;*
you loose your last
ounces of ammo,
aiming high,
hope-beyond-hoping

                    your Hail Mary
spans the expanse
                    and spatters accurate.
Time slow-mos;
                    the tossup torrent
swoops and bursts,
                    and, bingo!, bogies
go gaseous.
                    Guns without shooters
slap cement,
                    and the motile metals'
torpor continues.
                    Tick, tick, tick.
You pull up your partner,
                    pat her rump—
a human thing.


                    The throat-threatening
haze is heading
                    home to Hoboken.
All the aliens,
                    are they . . . ? Almost.
You spot, far-off,
                    through scraps of smoke,
the last thing lurking:
                    that lich Margaret
has pulled a console
                    from the com link's calf,
her tyrant tumors
                    tapping out, what,
a countdown code?
                    You can't get there,

can't fly. Guns dry,
                                your gung-ho go
at a bleach blitzkrieg
                                bombed big time.
The long-range colossus
                                is lighting up,
and you just stand there,
                                stupid, stung
by likely loss.


                        In lieu of leadership,
your only teammate
                        takes up the two
otherworldly weapons,
                                wings you one
and shouts, *Hey shithead,*
                                *shoot the mast.*
You shoot as told.
                        Your twin attractions
meet, marry,
                        and the Metro's most eminent
needle seeks
                        your magnetic north.
The strain screeches;
                                steel cables snap
and lash the night.
                                The leaning tower's
beacon blows;
                        the base buckles,
tears the long-range
                                totem's torso
loose of its legs.

                    Electric life
is bleeding out,
                    the brain bouncing
across concrete.

                    You kill the cannons,
sprint clear
                    of the spire's crash path.
True, there's time
                    to turn and love
watching this world's
                    unwelcomest guest
twist and face
                    titanic failure
moments before
                    the mast makes her
lizard mash.

                    The leveled landmark
juts toward Jersey,
                    judders, crumples.
The pendant part of it,
                    poised there over
ants idling
                    on Eighth Avenue,
frets awhile
                    but fails to fall.

Apollo's Dinerette. A vinyl booth
where you, the early birds who know the truth
about last night's iguana Waterloo,
are finishing a modest victory banquet.
The doc is spearing prune and honeydew;
you're pushing toast across your plate to sop
residual yolk. The mood is like the languid
morning after mad amounts of drugs.
The sunlight, like, could pass for cobalt blue,
and oil-slick rainbows undulate on top
of matching 'bottomless' ceramic mugs.

Apollo's Dinerette. A sticky booth
where you and What's Beside You, veteran youth,
sit mute among the dust motes, disinclined
to broach the future, but it doesn't matter.
(*Credence* churns the airwaves; ambient clatter
ebbs and flows.) Now that you share a mind
light years beyond the squint of humankind,
there's no big rush to stuff a hush with chatter.

(Student and agent, Mr. Either/Or,
you never trusted anyone before.)

Why shop for rocks? Why bother with a vow?
It's over: you're as good as married now.

# Books from Etruscan Press

# Etruscan Press is Proud of Support Received from

Wilkes University

Youngstown State University

The Ohio Arts Council

The Stephen & Jeryl Oristaglio Foundation

The Nathalie & James Andrews Foundation

The National Endowment for the Arts

The Ruth H. Beecher Foundation

The Bates-Manzano Fund

The New Mexico Community Foundation

Drs. Barbara Brothers & Gratia Murphy Fund

The Rayen Foundation

The Pella Corporation

The Raymond John Wean Foundation

Founded in 2001 with a generous grant from the Oristaglio Foundation, Etruscan Press is a nonprofit cooperative of poets and writers working to produce and promote books that nurture the dialogue among genres, achieve a distinctive voice, and reshape the literary and cultural histories of which we are a part.

etruscan press

www.etruscanpress.org

Etruscan Press books may be ordered from

Consortium Book Sales and Distribution

800.283.3572

www.cbsd.com

Etruscan Press is a 501(c)(3) nonprofit organization.
Contributions to Etruscan Press are tax deductible
as allowed under applicable law.
For more information, a prospectus,
or to order one of our titles,
contact us at books@etruscanpress.org.